PARANORMAL COZY MYSTERY

Wings & Broken Things

TRIXIE SILVERTALE

Sittin' On A Goldmine
Productions L.L.C.

Trixie Silvertale
Wings and Broken Things: Paranormal Cozy Mystery : a novel / by Trixie Silvertale — 1st ed.

[1. Paranormal Cozy Mystery — Fiction. 2. Cozy Mystery — Fiction. 3. Amateur Sleuths — Fiction. 4. Female Sleuth — Fiction. 5. Wit and Humor — Fiction.] 1. Title.

CHAPTER 1

THICK WHITE FLAKES float lazily toward my outstretched tongue. The inviting aroma of mulled
wine and cider drifts through the air and, for a moment, I almost put my arms out and spin. This must
be what it feels like to live inside a snow globe.

Except for the chainsaws.

Yes, you heard me correctly. Chainsaws.

At the indefatigable insistence of my volunteer
employee, Twiggy, I'm attending my first Northern
Lights Yuletide Extravaganza. Most people would
probably call it a winter carnival, but the good folks
at the Pin Cherry Harbor Chamber of Commerce
felt that the event needed more pizzazz.

Did you picture jazz-hands? Me too. However,
not mentioned in the invite is the fact that every
living soul in town is in attendance, despite the late

hour. And "late" in Pin Cherry is anything past 8:00 p.m. I'm sure the rest of our fair city looks like a ghost town.

As I stand next to the chainsaw ice-sculpture carving competition, I have to admit they definitely add the promised flair. Despite the ear-drum-blowing stuttering and revving of the saws, I am mesmerized by the beauty being revealed within eight-foot-by-three-foot columns of ice. The one of an angel almost seems to move its wings.

The magical fluttering of the giant flakes of ice dust makes me feel like I'm part of a Norse fairy-tale. All I need is a blonde-haired, blue-eyed Viking god to walk through the glittering mist—

"Erick?"

"Ah, Miss Moon, perhaps you are not as quick with names as I had hoped."

My disappointment is quickly replaced with a welcome surge of heat as the tall, dark, and green-eyed Rory Bombay scoops up my mittened hand and presses his lips to the thin wool. I can feel the intensity as clearly as if that stubble-kissed chin had touched my skin.

I let him thread my arm through his as I fall into step beside him. I'm not sure what brings him up north from his antiquities business in Grand Falls, but I'm not complaining. "Oh, Mr. Bombay, I remember your name. I was . . . it's not important."

"Please, call me Rory. And may I call you Mizithra?"

I want to blurt, "No you absolutely may not ever call me that," but his emerald eyes twinkle with mischief and I quickly retaliate. "Only if you'd like this to be our last date, Mr. Bombay."

His laughter swirls around me and I feel beautiful and sophisticated. The elation lasts an entire seven seconds before a huge baby stroller smacks into my knee and sends me sprawling on my ample behind in the snowbank beside the shoveled walkway.

The young mother's apology is swallowed by the screams of her drastically unhappy toddler.

A strong hand, clad in soft, black kidskin leather, reaches down. I grasp the lifeline and Rory Bombay pulls me up much too quickly. I crash into the firm planes of his chest and inhale sharply.

"I beg your pardon, Mitzy. Either you're light as a feather, or I don't know my own strength. I'm sure it would be the former." His full lips curve in a suggestive grin.

I should warn him that flattery will get him everywhere, but I'm trying to turn over a new leaf since I ran out on my flat-broke barista existence in Sedona, Arizona, for places so far north they could be mistaken for Canada.

"Is this your first Yuletide in Pin Cherry?" He

gently slips my arm through the crook of his as he inquires.

I like that he's jumping on the chamber's branding train. "Yes, I recently inherited the bookshop on Main Street and First Avenue from my grandmother and this will be my first winter here."

He clucks his tongue. "Oh dear. Are you prepared?" He slides my arm free and spins me out as though I'm his longtime ballroom dance partner. "Let's see. The boots look sufficient for an average winter, but if there's a blizzard like the one in '84 . . . The jeans are flattering, but you'll succumb to hypothermia in minutes when the true storms hit. You should definitely get a lovely pair of silk-lined snow pants."

I smile and play along. "What about the jacket?"

He pulls off his glove and rubs a section of my sleeve between his thumb and long artistic fingers. "Down is good, but this can't be rated for more than ten below. You'll need to upgrade before the solstice."

The word pricks the hairs on the back of my neck. I'm certain that if I slipped off my left mitten and looked at my recently deceased grandmother's magically enhanced mood ring some image would appear. Some kind of warning detected by my budding extra-sensory psychic powers. "Solstice?"

His smile holds a secret that vanishes like quicksilver. "I meant Christmas, of course. It can get down to seventy below zero in the heart of Jack Frost's realm." He scoops me back to his side and continues, "May I tell you a bit about this lovely time of year?"

"Of course."

"First stop, the glögg." He pauses at a booth and says, "Två."

The fresh-faced blonde with thick rabbit-fur earmuffs hands him two steaming mugs. He lays a fifty on the counter, nods, and picks up the two beverages. He does not ask for change.

With my work history as a transient barista, I have a deep appreciation for big tippers. I beam with genuine admiration as he hands me one of the drinks. "Do you speak Swedish?" I ask.

He chuckles. "Ah, you recognize your native tongue?"

I shake my head. "I'm not Swedish."

He looks at me with open appreciation. "Those eyes, grey as a winter storm cloud? That snow-white hair? You are not only Swedish, my darling. You are a Scandinavian goddess."

Despite the cold, my cheeks flush with heat.

"Let me show you to your palace, M'Lady." He leads me toward the lakeshore where a sparkle of lights like an enormous diamond dances through the snowfall.

"It's beautiful," I whisper.

"Come inside and try your glögg."

I follow him into the glowing structure constructed of thick blocks of ice, cut from the great lake that serves as the backdrop to this winter wonderland. The semi-transparent cubes sparkle from within. I take a long pull from my warm mug. "What is this?"

"Glögg means 'to burn or mull.' A brew that is lovingly crafted from old family recipes that include red wine, port, brandy, and spices. It is always served warm and is a favorite on St. Lucia's Day, but is, of course, delicious whenever the temperatures turn chilly."

I eagerly drain my mug in greedy gulps. The liquid trickles down my throat and warms my tummy. "It's delicious."

He clinks his mug to mine, takes a big swig, and continues, "Legends tell of King Gustav I Vasa of Sweden who created a warm drink made from German wine, sugar and spices. His drink was later named 'glödgag vin,' meaning 'glowing-hot wine.' The name eventually transformed to glögg by the late 1800s."

The warmth in my middle is spreading and creating a general softening of all my senses and I can't seem to tear my eyes away from the glögg-wet lips of the enticing Rory Bombay.

The sparkling lights.

The close quarters within the walls of the ice palace.

The deep thrum of his voice.

"Moon?"

That voice? I recognize the sound, but Rory's lips aren't moving.

"Moon, are you actually out socializing?" A friendly hand pats me on the back as though I'm part of some type of sports team.

My mulled brain sloshes a little as I turn. "Erick?"

Behind me, a disappointed sigh escapes my tour guide.

Erick steps rather close and the scent of my mulled wine is quickly replaced by the sharp citrus-woodsy smell of my secret crush. "Who's this?" He gestures to the man at my side.

I wait a beat while the scene plays out in my always-making-a-student-film mind. I sense a tinge of jealousy from Erick, even though he's never bothered to take me up on my blatant flirtatious advances. I have tripped and fallen on him at least three times, and he's saved my life twice, so maybe he thinks we're going steady. In my "mind movie" he slugs Rory in the jaw and tells him to keep his manicured hands off his girl. In reality, I introduce them. "Erick Harper, this is Rory Bombay, the new owner of Gershon Antiquities."

Rory steps forward and extends his hand. "Of course, it's Bombay Antiquities and Artifacts now."

Erick snags the outstretched hand and shakes it firmly several times. "And it's Sheriff Harper."

Even in my deliciously spiced state I pick up on the chill that settles over our trio when Erick adds his honorific to the mix.

"Always a pleasure to meet the local authorities, Sheriff." Rory recovers quickly and pulls his hand back.

The feeling passes and I wonder if Erick will offer to buy me a caramel apple. But before I can see my culinary dreams fulfilled his radio crackles to life. "Sheriff, we have a 962H on Pin Cherry Lane."

Erick depresses the button on the side of his mic. "10-4. En route."

I ask the question that is begging for an answer. "What's a 962H?"

The faint, possibly imagined, whisper of jealousy has vanished and Erick's striking face is tense with duty and a touch of worry. "Leave this to the authorities, Moon." He glances to my left. "Nice to meet you, Mr. Bombay. I'm sorry, but I have to respond to this call immediately."

"It was a pleasure, Sheriff Harper." Rory nods stiffly.

Erick tips his head in a way that insinuates a brim to his non-existent hat. "Enjoy your evening, Miss Moon."

I'm sure he knows there's virtually no chance of that happening now that my wheels are spinning. I can Google things, Erick. Maybe I'll buy myself a police-band radio. I mean, what's an heiress to do if not meddle in the affairs of her community—or at least her community's sexy sheriff.

Rory slips his arm around my waist and leans close to my ear. "Did I ever tell you about the time I survived a two-day blizzard by building an igloo?"

I don't even need my extra senses to pick up on Rory's desperate attempt to erase all memory of Erick from our evening. Maybe it's the mulled wine, or the Yuletide magic, or the mesmerizing twinkle of lights in the snow castle—whatever the reason—I snuggle into Rory's warmth and reply, "Where did you learn to build an igloo?"

CHAPTER 2

THE WEAK LIGHT of morning doesn't have a chance of rousing me from the deep sleep afforded by my flannel sheets, electric blanket, and thick down comforter.

However, the rude bomb of tan fur terrorizing my chest gets the job done effortlessly.

"Pyewacket!" I shove my grandmother's rescued caracal off, despite his history of saving my life. A girl's gratitude has limits—

I spin right and breathe a huge sigh of relief when I see my large bed is devoid of company. And, upon further inspection of the luxurious four-poster bed, I deduce that I slept alone. Lucky for me, because if Grams—

"Good morning, Mitzy. Are you wondering how you got here?"

The splash of recovering alcoholic's condescension in my ghost grandmother's voice does not escape my notice. I carefully clear my mind of all snark so that she won't have the usual satisfaction of reading my private thoughts. "Good morning to you, Myrtle Isadora Johnson Linder Duncan Willamet Rogers."

She scoffs and swirls toward the high, coffered ceiling.

You see, my dearly departed grandmother, previous owner of this swanky apartment and the three-story bookstore on the other side of my secret door, was a bit of a skank herself.

"Mizithra Achelois Moon!" Ghost-ma dives toward me in a fury. Clearly she's broken our "no thought-reading" rule.

"Takes one to know one, Grams."

"Well, I never."

"We both know you did. At least five times!" I guffaw loudly as I stumble toward the bathroom.

"How many times do I have to tell you, there's a big difference between a sk—"

"Grams, the only thing that made you a 'woman of means, who knows what she wants' was a few decimal points in your bank account."

"Tom-ay-to, tom-ah-to." She crosses her bejeweled limbs over her burgundy silk-and-tulle Marchesa gown and shakes her head. She may have passed away in her early sixties, but at her chosen ghost-age of thirty-five she looks like an aristocratic older sister.

"Don't I at least get some points for coming home alone?" I gesture magnanimously to my empty four-poster bed.

A mischievous light twinkles in her ethereal eyes as she floats down to my level. "Before you get too comfortable up on that high and mighty horse of yours, you might want to chat with Twiggy."

I swallow audibly. "Oh." You see, Twiggy is Grams' former best friend and my one and only employee, although she works for the entertainment not the cash. I would not be able to run the bookshop without her—and she knows it. I shudder to think what humiliation I will have to endure over my first cup of wake-up juice.

"RE-ow." Which is Pye-speak for "Feed me." I'm slowly but surely learning to decipher the subtle variations in his pointed mewing, and he seems to have no trouble understanding English, so we have a workable system.

"Come on, you bossy fur ball. Let's get your Fruity Puffs before someone loses a finger." I press the plaster circle of ivy vines above the intercom and the secret door from my apartment to the Rare Books Loft glides open.

Contrary to my normal morning stomp-shuffle,

I tiptoe across the thick carpeting of the loft and down the metal leaves of the spiral staircase. But before I can set a hesitant foot on the main floor—

"Mornin', doll. How's that glögg treating you?" Twiggy's cackle echoes off the tin-plated ceiling and bounces back toward my ears like tiny arrows laced with mockery's poison. Her arms are crossed over her flannel button-down and her helmet of grey hair does not move as she shakes with laughter.

"Fine," I mumble. And this is the entertainment of which I spoke.

"I hate to burst your bubble, but I think that slick-talkin' Bombay fella was a whole lot more interested in gettin' inside your bookshop than anything else."

More grating locker-room snickering.

I pour some liquid alert into a possibly clean mug and slump into a stiff wooden chair. As the caffeinated potion seeps into my veins a thought bubbles to the surface. "Wait, what?"

"By the time I bumped into you at the Yuletide Extravaganza, you were three sheets to the wind and he was workin' overtime trying to convince you he was a perfect gentleman and only wanted to 'safely escort you home.' Well, I told him to shove off and managed to get you home in one piece all by my little lonesome." A volley of chuckles.

I gulp down more java and respond, "I remember him being very courteous and I'm sure he would've walked me home like a gentleman if you hadn't interfered." I scowl at her across the rim of my mug. Now that I'm waking up, I recall how interested he was in my Rare Books Loft, and I've come to realize it's freezing in here. "I've got to get some warm clothes on and find a proper breakfast."

A quick trip to the closet later, and I'm stomping through the fresh snowfall on Main Street toward Myrtle's Diner in a thick hoodie that says, "Eat, Drink & Be Meowy." This should get a chuckle or two at breakfast. The more I get to know the owner, Odell Johnson, the happier I am that he and my grandmother reconciled in her final days. It seems like her life would've been quite different if she and Odell had stayed together. However, then I would never have been born or had the good fortune to wind up in Pin Cherry Harbor.

A large black industrial floor mat sits just inside the door, adorned with chunks of muddy snow and ice in various stages of liquefying. A quick glance around the quaint diner proves that last night's festivities were attended by plenty of out-of-towners, or tourons as I prefer to call them. Every red-vinyl booth is filled to bursting, and all of the low four-tops are taken as well. I spot an empty stool at the counter and make a beeline, before I lose my last chance at a hot breakfast.

The grey crew-cut-topped head of Odell pops into the orders-up window and he gives me the standard salute with his metal spatula. I've come to learn that there's no need to place an order. Odell prides himself on knowing exactly what people want. I reach out and my hand encounters an empty space where my cup of coffee usually sits. At this point, I realize the lively flame-red-bun-topped head of the best waitress in Pin Cherry is missing. I shout above the din of the bustling restaurant, "Where's Tally?"

"Not coming in today."

"Is she sick? Should I check on her?"

Odell shakes his head. Something in his expression plucks a nervous chord in my heart.

"Everything okay?" Before he can answer, the man next to me slips off his stool, folds his newspaper in half, and slaps it down on the counter before he walks out.

Odell nods toward the paper. It takes a moment for me to realize that I've never before read a newspaper. But now that I've left the new-age mecca of Sedona, Arizona, and the high-tech life of a barely employed barista, I guess I'll start reading the newspaper like a local. I pick up the copy of the *Pin Cherry Harbor Post* and smooth it out on the counter in front of me. There above the fold is a shocking headline.

LOCAL VET INVOLVED IN HIT AND RUN.

Knowing that Odell served as an Army cook back in the day, I look up, concerned that he's the veteran. He shakes his head and motions for me to keep reading. As my eyes scan over the dancing black letters, I see that our beloved veterinarian, Doc Ledo, was mysteriously struck down on his way home after a late-night emergency surgery on a local service animal. Worry washes over me, but before I can say anything Odell intervenes.

"Tally won't be in today. Went to check on her brother at the hospital. No news yet." His metal spatula scrapes across the grill and the lines in Odell's face seem to deepen with additional years of concern.

He walks out from the kitchen and puts a plate in front of me. Perfectly scrambled eggs and chorizo with a side of deliciously browned home fries. He spins around and fills a mug with coffee, setting it down in front of me and emptying the pot down the row of waiting cups at the counter.

I gobble down my breakfast and chug the coffee. Wiping my mouth on a napkin, I bus my own dishes and make a fresh pot of coffee. The door scrapes open and two more patrons enter.

Snagging a couple menus from the stack, I show the new patrons to the recently vacated stools at the counter. As soon as the fresh pot of coffee is ready I make a round, filling cups and fetching to-go boxes.

When I return the pot to the coffee maker and brew up another round of black gold, I catch Odell smiling as he works. I lean on the ledge of the orders-up window and say, "I was just a poor working stiff before Grams left me a bookstore and a pile of cash."

He chuckles and replies, "Thanks."

It takes a little finagling to figure out the "no-tech" cash register, but before long the dwindling breakfast crowd turns into the lunch rush and the next time I look up it's nearly three o'clock in the afternoon and Odell is serving up a piece of pie topped with creamy vanilla ice cream.

"Hey, you better take your state-mandated break." He sets the pie on the counter and fills a fresh mug with coffee.

"Still the best pin cherry pie in town."

"The tourists should all be back on the road by now. I'd sure appreciate it if you could check on Tally. You know she's awful close to her big brother, Ledo. I can't imagine how upset she must be."

"Hit and run? In this town? Do they have any leads?"

I should be offended by the rumbling laughter coming from Odell, but it's to be expected.

"Seems like you're getting yourself quite a reputation in this town. You planning on running for sheriff?"

"No thank you. I prefer to stick my nose where it *doesn't* belong and actually solve cases."

We share a laugh and I greedily finish my pie. "Maybe I'll stop by the station on my way to the hospital."

"Sounds like Mitzy Moon is on the case." Odell chuckles as he clears my plate and I head out to see what I can uncover about the driver who struck down the man who saved Pyewacket's life.

Outside, the sidewalk resembles a poorly designed checkerboard. Some sections are shoveled clean and sprinkled with salt, which I've learned prevents ice from forming on the concrete when the temperatures inevitably drop below zero as the sun sets. But in front of the abandoned or closed businesses, the snow is piled high. So I play an unwelcome game of hopscotch as I make my way to the sheriff's station. But as luck would have it my incredible coordination betrays me at precisely the most inopportune moment.

I hop up and over an un-shoveled section of sidewalk, but instead of landing on a lovely shoveled square with a generous sprinkling of salty grit, my foot hits a perfectly slick patch of icy terror. One foot goes left, the other goes north, and before I know what's hit me, I'm on my back in the man-made snowdrift left by the plow the night before. Flailing like a turtle on its shell, I desperately seek some purchase in the deep snow. My suffering is put to an end as two strong hands grip my waving arms and pull me to my feet.

"Oh my," I manage to utter by way of a thank you. I don't think I've ever been this close to Erick without having tripped and fallen on top of him! I can actually feel the heat of his body through his thick winter uniform jacket. I have an inexplicable urge to lick the word "SHERIFF" on his badge, but even in Arizona the legends of tongues sticking to things in the frozen north had reached my ears—so I manage to control myself.

"You might want to consider attending a survival course, Miss Moon. I realize this is your first real winter, and we wouldn't want you freezing to death simply because you don't know how to get out of a snowbank." He barely has the decency to finish the sentence before he's gripped by uncontrollable belly laughs.

I choose to press the only advantage I've ever had and step closer to the luscious blonde-haired, blue-eyed Sheriff Erick Harper. "Are you offering me private lessons, Erick?"

He shuffles backward, falters on the same patch of ice that claimed me, but somehow manages to keep his feet underneath him. He clears his throat nervously and offers another round of sound advice. "You be careful out there, Miss Moon. And get yourself some thermal long johns or some snow pants. You'll freeze to death in no time in those jeans."

I'm definitely flattered that he's looking at my jeans, but I have a job to do. "I'm on my way to see Tally. Can I let her know if you have any leads on the driver of the car that struck her brother?"

A pained expression grips Erick's face and he shakes his head solemnly. "It's a real shame about Ledo. He's a great guy and has always been more than fair about taking care of pets, even when families fall on hard times. He saved my little Casserole's leg and wouldn't even let me pay him extra for coming in on a Sunday."

There are so many things to unpack in that statement, I don't know where to begin. But, let's be honest, we both want to know the same thing. "Is Casserole a cat or a dog?"

Erick blushes, looks down at his boot, and kicks at some frozen chunks of dirty snow left behind by the plow. "Casserole was a potbelly pig."

"Was? Was Casserole's name a self-fulfilling prophecy?"

Erick looks up, and his steel-blue eyes soften with memory as a warm smile spreads across his face.

I can feel my heart melting inside my chest like an icicle in the sun.

"Casserole died of natural causes when I was on my second tour in Afghanistan." For a moment there is a flash of pain, but it vanishes quicker than a lightning strike, and the muscles in Erick's cheeks flex as he clenches his jaw and hardens his expression.

"Sounds like a long story. Maybe you'll tell me over a slice of pin cherry pie sometime . . ."

Erick gives a noncommittal shrug.

"Do you have anything on the driver?" I figure it can't hurt to ask again.

"I feel like I'd be wasting my breath if I told you to stay out of this, Moon. But rest assured that I will find out who did this to Doc Ledo, and I'll make sure they pay."

The hard edge in Erick's voice and the menacing energy drifting off him in waves sends a very non-wintry chill down my spine. Beneath that soft "Andy Taylor" folksy exterior lurks a soldier who's had to make hard decisions, and will make them again.

"Good day, Moon."

As the delicious distraction that is Erick stalks down the street toward his cruiser, I become uncomfortably aware of the melting snow trickling down the inside of my boots and possibly even my pants.

In addition to the freezing wetness, my feet are throbbing with fatigue. Looks like my life of leisure in Pin Cherry has softened my edge. After a busy day on my feet at the diner, all I can think of is a long hot bath and my cozy bed.

Seems like my trip to the hospital can wait until tomorrow.

CHAPTER 3

HAVING HAD the unique experience of reading the local paper yesterday, I decide for a repeat with to-day's breakfast. There are only three of us at Myrtle's Diner this morning, and someone has abandoned his or her paper at one of the four-tops. I pick it up, slide into a booth, and smooth it out on the silver-flecked white Formica table. Top story: MISSING ANGEL BREAKS WIDOW'S HEART

It seems that a three-foot-high memorial statue containing the ashes of Oslo Jorgensen was stolen from the front porch of Olga Jorgensen on Saturday night. The article goes on to explain that the angel was a custom-ordered memorial, which contained the ashes of the woman's dearly departed husband.

The inscription read, "On angel's wings you were borne away, but in my heart you shall always stay."

I lean back and take a long, comforting sip of my hot java. Who would steal a memorial? Did they know the husband's ashes were inside? Is it vandalism or just theft? There's no photo of the stolen statuary, but the image that accompanies the story is far more haunting: just footprints in the snow, leading away from her house. Reminds me of a poem, however this time it would appear the thief carried the angel. There is some sort of marking—

Tally slides my plate onto the table and interrupts my musings.

I inhale deeply. "That smells delicious. I think Odell was seriously off his game without you yesterday. I know he's happy to have you back. How's Ledo doing?"

Tally nods her head rapidly and the tight flame-red bun perched on top bobs with it. "He's doing real good, you know? The doctors say—" Her voice catches in her throat and I put a hand on her arm.

"I didn't mean to upset you, Tally. I'm so sorry about what happened. I know they're doing everything they can for him. And I heard that one of the veterinarians over in Broken Rock is going to come up twice a week until Ledo's back on his feet." I realize my mistake too late.

Tally's eyes fill with tears and she scurries into the back room.

I want to smack my forehead on the table. Back on his feet! Such an idiot! The poor doctor will probably be paralyzed from the waist down because of the thoughtless motorist who left him to die in the street, and I say "back on his feet." I suddenly lose my appetite.

Odell wanders out from the kitchen and quietly slips onto the bench seat across the table from me. "Don't beat yourself up kid, Tally knows you mean well. Ledo's always taken care of her. It's gonna take a while."

I lean forward and whisper, "I feel like such an idiot."

"Don't sweat it. Eat your breakfast and then go figure out who did this to him. That's the best thing you can do for Tally right now." Odell slides out of the booth, raps his knuckles on the table twice, and saunters back into the kitchen.

He's right. That's the best thing I can do for Tally right now. A good portion of my appetite is restored by Odell's encouraging words. I eat half my scrambled eggs and all my home fries. Draining the last of my coffee, I nod my thanks and walk out of the diner.

On my return trip to the bookshop, I notice all the footprints in the packed snow covering the sidewalk. Mostly different deep-treaded winter boots, I guess. But there's the occasional smooth-soled dress shoe and, of course, my tennis shoes with their cheap generic logo in the arch—

That's what it was! The marking left by that shoe in the snow. The photo in the paper wasn't very clear, but maybe if I go down to the *Pin Cherry Harbor Post*'s main office, I can get a look at the original digital file. Maybe even enlarge it. I mean, on TV they can enlarge images a thousand percent without any loss of resolution, so it can't be that hard. If I can see what brand of shoes the thief was wearing, then I can figure out who stole that angel.

Hold on! I don't have time to get involved in statuary theft. I need to stay focused and figure out who could run a man down in the middle of a snowstorm and leave him for dead on the road. That's my primary mission.

After I change my clothes and add a proper winter coat, Grams informs me that I'll have to take the Jeep.

Having one car was news to me, but learning that one does not drive one's 1957 Mercedes 300SL with gullwing doors during the winter months . . . mind blown.

"And where will I find this Jeep?"

"It's two garages down—toward the lake—from the Mercedes. Same access code."

"Do I want to know what's in that middle garage, or do I have to wait for another season?"

Grams laughs and shakes her head. "I honestly don't remember. It might be artwork, or books, or maybe clothes?" She floats lazily toward the window and gazes out over the frozen lake. "I think some of my life is getting fuzzy, Mitzy. Do you think that's how it starts? First I forget a couple harmless details and eventually it's all gone?"

Her tone worries me. "Grams, come on. You said yourself: you're well and truly stuck here. I think the dead only vanish once they're forgotten, and I'm still getting to know you. So what if you forgot the contents of one of your ancillary garages? You're here. I'm here. What is it you always say? One day at a time. Right?"

Tears spring from her eyes as she closes the distance between us. "Oh, Mitzy, I don't deserve you!"

I awkwardly give her a ghost-hug. "Until I can figure out a way to get you an afterlife handkerchief, I'd call us even. Deal?"

She snuffles and wipes at her translucent cheeks. "Deal."

"I'm off to the hospital. Wish me luck." I casually wonder where the keys are to my "other" car?

"Keys are tucked in the visor."

I almost point to my lips and scold her for

thought-dropping, but I did actually need an answer to that unspoken question.

As much as it pains me to admit it, the best place to start my investigation of the hit and run is by interviewing the sole witness to the crime. Unfortunately, I've always had a strong aversion to illness and hospitals. It's not that I personally have any issue with sick people, but growing up in foster care has left me with a general distrust of institutions. I had been living with foster mom number three and finally finding a tiny bit of comfort after my mother's fatal car accident when I got jumped by a gang of kids on my way home from school. They had only meant to frighten me, but my fight or flight instinct was stuck on "high alert" and I overreacted. I ran like a girl possessed and tripped and fell down an embankment. In addition to the cuts and bruises, I broke my left arm. I never found out who called the ambulance, but when I woke up in the hospital there were two policemen and a woman from Child Protective Services discussing my new placement. Foster family number four was unquestionably one of the worst experiences of my young life. And ever since, I've been less than thrilled with hospitals. However, I'm a big girl now, so I better put on my big-girl pants, get over to the hospital, and see if Ledo can remember anything.

Despite my courageous pep talk on the drive

WINGS AND BROKEN THINGS / 29

over, my lack of confidence with winter driving, combined with unpleasant childhood memories, produces a state of agitation by the time I arrive at the Birch County Regional Medical Facility.

As I approach the nurses' station I hesitate and worry they might not let me in, because I'm not family. Before I can make my cowardly exit, the friendly, efficient woman behind the counter notices me.

"Who are you here to see, Miss?"

"Dr. Toledo." My voice lacks any of the confidence necessary to convince her I'm a relative. And at that moment, I also realize I have no idea of the doctor's last name. Just a funny anecdote about how he and his sisters are all named after the towns of their conceptions. A story shared by Twiggy—possibly untrue and definitely inappropriate for this setting.

"And your pet's name?"

My jaw drops, and I gape at the woman for a solid ten seconds. "My what?"

She chuckles. "Ledo has had visits from several pet owners . . . It seems that he's better at remembering the pet's names than their people's. So he's asked us to introduce his guests by the name of their furry friends, or feathered."

I smile and nod. It would appear I'm not the

only person who likes to put things in context. "The name is Pyewacket."

The nurse smiles and nods her approval. "Great name." She walks out from behind the desk and gestures for me to follow.

We make our way down the hall and turn into a room so festooned with flower arrangements that I worry she may have directed me to the hospital gift shop rather than Ledo's room.

"Well, Ledo, it looks like you have another visitor. This one is Pyewacket." The nurse waves her arm magnanimously toward the man in the hospital bed. I mumble my thanks and move hesitantly toward the figure.

"Mitzy Moon! It's so nice of you to visit. I'd get up, but they tell me the legs have gone into early retirement—possibly, permanently."

"I'm sorry." I mumble and avoid his eyes. I don't know what to say. I shouldn't have come.

"Don't be sorry. Look at all the folks who care about me." He carefully gestures to the bouquets.

I glance around the room at the overabundance of flower arrangements and realize how much this man is loved, how little my visit truly matters, and how sweet it is of him to pretend that it does. I thrust a box of Fruity Puffs in his general direction and say, "It's what Pyewacket wanted you to have."

He laughs and then clutches his chest. "Three broken ribs. Don't make me laugh."

"I'm so sorry!"

He gently lifts his arm and takes the box of Fruity Puffs. "No need to apologize, Mitzy. I needed that laugh. And I really need this box of Fruity Puffs. As you can see, I have more flowers than I know what to do with. In fact, could you do me a favor?"

"Absolutely. Can I get you some water or coffee?"

He grips his chest and chuckles quietly. "Now you sound like Tally."

We both laugh a little about that.

"I was actually wondering if you would take these flowers and distribute them at the pet cemetery?"

"We have a pet cemetery?" All I can think of is the horrifying movie, and I have great concern for my personal safety.

Seeming to read my mind, he replies, "It's nothing like the movie. It's just a lovely place where people can remember the unconditional love that their pets provided. The Pin Cherry Harbor Welcoming Committee and the Ladies Luncheon League run a couple of fundraisers every year to pay the property taxes and a part-time groundskeeper. But I have no use for all these flowers and it would certainly brighten the place up. At least for a few hours, before the blooms freeze. But, maybe you could get the paper to take some photos and then the joy will last forever."

I'm speechless. I look at this man who may never regain the use of his legs and I can't comprehend how, even in what seems like his darkest hour, his first thought is for others. A wave of guilt washes over me. My self-absorbed, misspent youth can't be relived, but I am absolutely going to distribute these beautiful flowers and set up a photo shoot with the local paper. And then I'm going to drive to my lawyer's office and set up a philanthropic organization, finally. Mitzy Moon is going to make some attempt to leave the world a better place than she found it.

"Mitzy? Everything okay?"

I surface from my existential dive and reply, "I'm supposed to be here to cheer you up." I force a smile to my face and give my personality an injection of artificial sunshine.

Ledo tilts his head and stares at me wistfully. "You don't have to use kid gloves around me, dear. I know the extent of my injuries and I know the odds are not in my favor. But I didn't suffer any brain damage and I have full use of my hands and fingers. There will be an adjustment period as I get used to life in a wheelchair, but I can still practice medicine. I can still help all my patients, and that's what's truly important to me."

I nod my head, but still can't find my voice.

"I'm not going to pretend it will be easy. I know there are dark days ahead. But I'm not giving up. Giving up is a one-way ticket to somewhere I don't want to go."

"Ledo, I will absolutely take these flowers anywhere you want them to be. And if it's all right with you, I'd also like to find the person who did this to you."

"Well now." He chuckles carefully. "I've heard some mighty fine stories about amateur sleuth Mitzy Moon. Seems like you've done more than your share of legwork for the sheriff since you came into town. When Tally was here yesterday, she couldn't stop talking about how you'd helped Odell get to the bottom of Walt's murder and even got some leniency for little Diane. I'm not interested in retribution or vengeance, but I wouldn't mind making sure someone has to face the music."

"Exactly what I was thinking." I slide a chair closer to the bed, sit down, and pull out my phone in case I need to take notes. "Tell me everything you remember, even if it doesn't seem important."

As Ledo relives the painful memories of the night he was struck down, I keep a careful watch on my grandmother's mood ring on my left hand. Unfortunately, nothing in his tale offers any clue to what might've happened, and he seems to have no memory of the shape, size, or color of the vehicle that hit him. The Doc had been looking down at his phone, searching for the right "walking home" playlist when he stepped into the street without looking and was hit almost instantly.

"Did the vehicle try to stop? Did you hear brakes screech?"

"I honestly don't remember. But even if they had tried to stop . . . with the snow falling . . . the slippery roads . . . I'm sure they did everything they could."

This must be what it's like to talk to the Dalai Lama. The man seems genuinely at peace with what happened. "Can you remember anything else?"

"The doctor here said I might be missing a few memories. I did hit my head and there was a mild concussion, but nothing serious. There's a chance a memory or two may have been dashed away by the pavement, but if I think of anything else I'll for sure let you know."

"All right. I'll start poking around, and get these flowers transported over to the pet cemetery while I organize the photo shoot." I turn to survey the vast array of bouquets and mentally power through a series of options for getting them moved. Behind me, I hear the sound of cardboard tearing, plastic ripping, and a loud crunch followed by a satisfied murmur. I turn around just in time to see Ledo reaching in for a second handful of Fruity Puffs.

"I can see why Pyewacket loves these things. You'll give him my best, won't you?"

"I absolutely will." Gesturing to the arrangements, I ask, "Do you want all of them moved or just certain ones?"

"I'll keep this Winter Wonderland arrangement from Tally and Tilly." He points to a beautiful selection of holly leaves, red berries, pinecones, and silver bells arranged around a snow globe. "But all the rest of them are fair game, you know?"

I nod and begin making a rough calculation of how much space will be needed.

"And when you're talking to the paper, maybe you can ask them to run an article requesting donations to the pet cemetery in lieu of flowers, so we can prevent a second floral apocalypse." He laughs at his own joke and clutches his fractured ribs once more.

"You're not doing yourself any favors, Doc." I chuckle. "I'm on the case."

Having slowly come to terms with the benefits of my inheritance, I call the local florist and offer to hire them to relocate all of the bouquets to the pet cemetery. They happily quote me a price and agree to handle it the very next day. My second phone call is to the local paper, informing them of a wonderful winter photo opportunity and purchasing a half-page, full-color ad offering a reward for anyone who has information about the hit and run to call in with tips—with a note at the bottom asking for donations to the pet cemetery in lieu of flowers. That completes my transaction with our local news outlet.

Now it's time for me to finally sit down with my attorney, Silas Willoughby—who happens to be an alchemist—and set up an organization designed to give back to this community, which I've decided to call home. And of course, I'll see what he can do about getting a copy of the police report so that I can peruse the details of Ledo's accident.

Despite Ledo's calm and friendly nature, the smells and sounds of the hospital are giving me a mild case of the heebie-jeebies. "I better get started on these errands. You let me know if you need any more Fruity Puffs, all right?"

"You betcha!" Ledo stifles a snicker and squeezes his ribs.

CHAPTER 4

AFTER STOPPING by the bank to withdraw cash and update Tilly, the oldest of the three, on her brother's floral directives, I drive to the newspaper. Apparently, the only place in town that accepts electronic payments is the florist. Everywhere else deals in cash, as though I'm trapped in an old pre-tech-revolution alternate dimension. I mean, I have a passbook in which they type my deposits and withdrawals—with a typewriter! Sometimes I wonder if I'm even in color.

I'm hoping that the heartwarming human-interest story on Doc Ledo, combined with the big ad purchase, will grease the wheels at the *Pin Cherry Harbor Post.*

As soon as I enter the old brick building, which houses the local paper, I can smell the ink. It reminds me of my bookshop, but in a raw, straight-to-the-source kind of way. I approach the birch-clad reception area and ring the bell, which squats below a sign instructing me to do just that.

A kid that looks roughly high-school age wanders out of a back room and nods.

I feel old as I assume that's what passes for a greeting with his generation. "Hi, I'm Mitzy. I purchased—"

"Oh, right. The ad. Sit tight."

Rude. I shudder to think how many coffee-shop patrons I've offended over the years. So, if you're wondering, I'm the pot, not the kettle.

I fish my formerly crisp twenties out of my pocket and continue to "sit tight."

Mr. Manners pauses his rustling of papers and yells, "Dad! Dad, the lady is here about the giant ad." He rolls his eyes and exhales, before turning and walking into the back without so much as a "by your leave."

The next human to burst from the bowels of this journalistic house of integrity is both smaller and more bespectacled than I could ever have dreamed. The man is possibly five feet tall in boots, and his eyewear looks as though it was stolen from a prop comic's trunk.

An ink-stained hand thrusts itself in my general direction. "Miss Moon, sorry about Quince. He's great behind the camera, but not all that comfort-able with people."

"Your son is the photographer?"

He nods furiously.

Just my luck. I can't wait to try and pry informa-tion out of that "Chatty Cathy."

"I'm sorry I didn't have time to tell you on the phone, but we don't have 'full-color' ads. We're a one-color press operation. Not that we wouldn't love to run color, but our old Heidelberg just keeps whirring away, so it looks like we won't be up-grading to a 2- or 4-color press anytime soon. Not that we could afford it with subscriptions waning and the bloggers scooping all our stories. But, you know, we've been in the newspaper business since my great-great-grandmother moved here and mar-ried into the Knudsen family in 1869 . . ."

In case you were wondering, he's still shaking my hand. I twist my hand away as politely as pos-sible and make a desperate attempt to staunch the flow of words spilling from his face. "Wow! What a story. Listen, the one-color ad is fine. I'll go ahead and purchase a two-page spread to draw more at-tention to the information. What do I owe you?"

His enlarged eyes blink behind his enormous lenses like a confused frog.

I start peeling twenties off the roll in my hand. "Is a hundred dollars enough?"

Blink. Blink. Blink.

"Two hundred?"

"Two hundred is good." Look who suddenly returned!

Quince for the win. I have a sneaking suspicion that two hundred is far too much, but at this point I just want to end this transaction.

"Here you go." I lay the bills on the ink-smudged counter and turn to leave. Luckily a tingle on my ring finger reminds me that I had a second reason for my blatant bribery of the fourth estate. Rounding on Quince, I ask, "Did you take that pic of the footprint in the snow?"

His hands scoop up the cash guiltily before he answers. "Yah."

"You still got the original?"

"Yah."

At least I know this kid's currency. "How much?"

His eyes narrow in confusion.

"How much for the pic? I'll buy it off you right now. You text it to me and I'll pay you."

Something in my short speech has awakened the transfixed patriarch. "Quince doesn't shoot digital. He has an SLR and develops—"

I put my hands up in surrender, because I don't need a history lesson on the invention of the *camera obscura* by Leonardo da Vinci. I'm a film-school

dropout, remember? "Awesome. Can I buy the negative and an enlarged print?"

Blink. Blink. Blink.

"Yah. Follow me, dude."

I guess I'm the "dude" in this scenario. I follow
the verbose young Quince to a black cylinder,
which he spins to reveal a revolving door.

He steps in and I move to follow. He flinches at
my nearness and mumbles, "One at a time."

I chuckle as the cylinder rotates and reopens to
reveal an empty tube. It's like a magician's trick. I'm
fascinated. I step into the tube and rotate the door
around me. A sliver of red light expands to fill the
barrel as the powerful odor of acids and ammonia
hits me.

"Sweet." Again I feel the weight of my age. This
guy is probably no more than five years younger
than me. Why do I feel as out of place as Arnold
Schwarzenegger in *Kindergarten Cop*?

He pulls strips of hanging film out and peers at
the negative images.

"Who taught you to do all this?"

"YouTube."

If he and his dad put all their words in a giant
lottery spinner and took turns pulling them out . . .
"Do you have that footprint pic?"

"You want 'em all?"

"All?"

"I took a bunch of exposures."

"Sure. I'll take all the negatives, but I need you to print out the best one at like 8″ x 10." I have no idea what sizes are standard, but I remember that one from school picture packets. Packets which were never purchased after my mom died because, let's face it, not a lot of foster families want to blow money on orphan pictures for no one.

"They're DCs."

"The photos?"

"The shoes." He unclips the strip of negatives, rolls it up, slips it into a little plastic canister, and hands it to me. "You're the PI, right?"

I spin the film canister in my hand and smile. "I just own the bookshop."

He nods. "I feel ya."

I grin. "DCs, huh?"

"Yah."

"What do I owe you?"

"Depends."

"Depends? On what?"

"You want me to tell Sheriff Harper I sold those"—he gestures toward the negatives—"or did I just lose 'em."

I think I'm getting hustled, and this kid is as good as Emma Stone in *Easy A*. "You look pretty absentminded."

"A hundred."

I count out five twenties, pause, and add two more. "Maybe we never met."

He takes the money a little too eagerly for a truly seasoned gangster.

I nod and slip out through the second-most awesome door in Pin Cherry Harbor. Slick as it is, this darkroom door cannot compete with my secret bookcase door.

I smile at the elder Knudsen as I walk out.

"Quince find that photo for you?"

I expertly palm the canister and shake my head. "He couldn't find the negatives."

"Kids these days . . ."

Whatever else he mumbles is lost to the closing front door.

CHAPTER 5

THE WEATHER HAS TRULY TURNED frightful. I
saw a sprinkling or two of snow in Sedona, but the
temperatures never dropped below zero. As I rush
to my car, I can actually feel my eyelashes freezing
together.

The heavy door on my four-wheel-drive Jeep
sticks a little in the cold, and I whimper as my
aching fingers struggle to get a grasp on the frosty
handle.

Once the door clicks shut I expect to feel better,
but my car has been chilling in the elements for
nearly twenty minutes.

I start the engine and fumble my stiff fingers
over the dials in a feeble attempt to get hot air
pumping through the vents. Lesson number one of

my first winter in almost-Canada: just because you turn the spinny knob to heat doesn't mean you will feel actual warmth.

Snow is falling in earnest now and I can no longer see the centerline on Main Street. I suddenly understand why Grams insisted I have a "winter" car and leave the sporty Mercedes 300SL in a nice dry garage until spring.

By the time I pull up in front of the bookshop, a tepid breeze is blowing across my frostbitten knuckles. I shove the shifter into park and run stiffly toward the intricately carved wooden door. My cold fingers cannot grasp the key and, after dropping it in the snow twice, I bang on the door and shout for my Ghost-ma.

Images from the terrifying *To Build a Fire* flash through my mind and panic grips my chest. I'll surely freeze to death right here on my own front stoop—

The slow scrape of metal tumblers interrupts my nightmare.

"Grams? Grams is that you?"

The door pushes open and knocks me on my backside, scrambling to retrieve the key.

The familiar cackle of Twiggy welcomes me home. "You thought a ghost was opening the door? Maybe you are suffering a little Arctic hallucination, doll." She stoops and picks up the key, but offers me no further assistance.

I struggle to my feet in a most unladylike fashion and dive into the relative warmth of the store. "Wh-what are-are you st-still doing here?" I force the words out between my chattering teeth.

Twiggy hands me the key and walks into the back room. She slips into her coat, hat, mittens, and scarf, before turning off the lights. "I was just leaving."

I watch her leave through the side door and scoff, as it slams shut. "She was waiting for me to get back and she likes me and worries about me, whether she wants to admit it or not."

"I agree, dear."

And there goes my bladder, folks.

Grams snickers into her bejeweled hand. "Sorry, honey. Pye and I were worried about you, so I came as soon as I heard you talking to Twiggy. I thought you sensed me."

"I can't even sense my own fingers right now!" I shake with a fresh wave of shivers.

"You take a nice hot shower and you'll feel warmer than a tea cozy."

I open my mouth to protest, but the mere thought of that miraculous shower and its consistently hot water is already making me feel better.

After an undisclosed amount of time thawing my frozen body in the luxurious steam-shower, I slip into my reindeer onesie and wrap a thick towel around my hair. I make a beeline for the inviting four-poster bed and bury myself under the double-thick down comforter.

Pye seems to sense my need for warmth and curls up on top of the covers, adding his significant weight as another blanket.

My fingers and toes appear intact, and my involuntary muscular convulsions have finally ceased. I'd be lying if I said I was looking forward to ever getting out of this bed, but at least nothing was actually lost to frostbite.

"Frostbite isn't nearly—"

I put up a hand for Grams to cease and desist, while I point meaningfully to my lips with the other hand.

"Of course, dear. I'm just glad you made it home safe, you know?"

"Do you know anything about shoes, Grams?"

"Jimmy Choo, Alexander McQueen, Christian Louboutin, Manolo Blahnik—"

My gasping laughter interrupts my fashion-horse grandmother's list of favorite things. "Um, no. I'm actually more interested in skateboard shoes."

"Oh, Mitzy, you're such a card! What would I

know about skateboard shoes? I took a walk or two on the wild side, but I never rode a scooter there."

"A couple of my foster brothers had some skills, but they never included me."

Grams brow furrows with concern. "What's the sudden interest in skateboarding in the winter, dear?"

I shake my head. "I'm sure it's nothing. But every time I think about that photo in the newspaper of the footprint in the snow, I get a feeling—"

She swirls over the bed and Pyewacket bristles as she drifts through him. "Is it your gifts? Are you getting a message?"

"No idea." I relay the story of visiting Ledo, arranging to have the flowers relocated, and then my strange interaction with the teen "blackmailer" who works as a photographer for the newspaper.

"Well, I think the boy sounds very industrious."

"That's one word for it."

"Did he know anyone with shoes like that? Those BCs, or whatever."

"They were DCs, Grams. I'm sure every kid at his—" I leap out of bed so fast I upend Pyewacket.

His retribution rips a tiny hole in the leg of my pajamas.

"Sorry, Pye. You'll absolutely forgive me when you hear my brilliant idea."

He turns away and does a yoga pose named for

his least favorite animal, so I'll simply mention it's a downward "D-word" to avoid losing a chunk of flesh. I take the insulting display of his rear end, pointed in my general direction, in stride.

"What idea? What are you talking about? Is this about the case?" Grams is swirling around me like a Ghost-ma merry-go-round.

"It's about an article I read in the paper."

"You read the paper? I thought your generation was all about the blogging and what not."

I strike an indignant pose, but before I can utter my witty retort Grams belly laughs uncontrollably.

"What's so funny?"

"I know I'm not supposed to read your mind or listen to your thoughts, or whatever this is, but when you . . . those pajamas . . . it just tickled me."

I have to admit I probably don't look super in-timidating with a furry belly and little brown antlers hanging off each side of the hood. "Can we get back to my brilliant idea?"

"Of course." She continues to snicker and wipes laughter tears from the corners of her eyes.

"I was about to say that probably every kid at his high school has those shoes. So, what better way to track down the owner of this particular pair of DCs than to go to the high school?"

Grams grows unusually quiet and her eyes dart left and right.

"What's going on? Was the principal of the high school one of your 'special friends?' Did you burn a bridge?"

She floats toward me with a look of morose pity flickering across her face. "You know I love you, Mitzy, and you know I think you are just the most beautiful girl in the whole world, but you can't pass for a high-school girl, sweetie." Her ethereal hand reaches out and I feel the comfort of her energy on my shoulder.

"I'm not going to pass myself off as a student, Grams. Well, not a high-school student." I wink meaningfully.

Her aura lights up like a Christmas tree. "The Birch County Community College!"

I nod and smile as I flash my eyebrows mischievously. "I'm thinking some kind of psychology student who needs to complete a certain number of observation hours or something."

"You swipe it up on your phone and get your backstory straight while I select your character's wardrobe."

"My character's wardrobe? My backstory? Who are you right now?"

"You know I used to write screenplays, dear. Just because I never sold one to a big Hollywood producer doesn't mean I don't know how to dress a set." She giggles like a schoolgirl as she zooms into the closet.

I'll leave her to work her magic in a closet that can only be described as right out of *Sex and the City* meets *Confessions of a Shopaholic*. While I work on my "backstory."

CHAPTER 6

As you may or may not know, I am not a morning person. I do not like bright sun in my face. I do not like rushing all over the place. I do not like it with a ghost. I do not like it with cold toast.

But, today is my first day of undercover work at the school and despite my aversion to the ungodly hour of 7:00 a.m., I'm managing to pull together a "look" that Grams assures me will win the day.

"Do you have your notebook?"

"Kids just record their lessons these days, Grams. I've got my phone. That should cover everything."

"What's your name?"

I spin on my chunky-heeled boots and grin. "Darcy Brown."

She squeals and claps her hands. "Good luck, Darcy!"

I chuckle as I slip out of the apartment and speak the school's address into my phone.

The fifteen-minute drive is a breeze on the newly plowed streets. I turn into the high-school parking lot and take a moment to survey my surroundings while I pluck up my courage.

Busses are pulling into the half-circle drive in front of the school. The students are unloading in a chaotic stream of pushing, shouting, and occasionally, snowball throwing. I think I'll wait right here until the bell rings. I have no interest in this *Lord of the Flies* nonsense.

BRRRRRRRING!

The earsplitting bell drives the children inside. I wait until the aides who monitor the drop-off zone sweep up all the stragglers, and I carefully make my way to the office.

There's a vivacious blonde waif at the counter in a heated exchange with a woman bearing the nametag, "Donna Jo – Secretary."

"But Donna Jo, you know my mom can't drive good in the snow. It's like, not my fault I'm late."

"Can't drive well, Brynley. I'm sure you'd know that if you weren't late to English every single day. I'll write you a pass and I will add your name to the detention roster."

"That sucks!"

"Language, Brynley."

"Principal Puig took my phone and, like, I can't even call my mom. She's gonna be super pissed—"

Donna Jo's face transforms from mildly irritated school secretary to avenging angel in a split second. "I think maybe we need to have a chat with Principal Puig right now, young lady."

I chew the inside of my cheek to keep from snickering. The sheer number of times I've been referred to as "young lady" in a school office . . . No need to dredge up the past. I'm no longer wayward foster child, Mitzy Moon. I'm—

"May I help you, dear?"

A kind, elderly lady labeled "Mrs. Boulton – School Nurse" has replaced the over-reaching Donna Jo. I thank the spirits for my good fortune and step up to the counter.

"I'm Darcy Brown. I'm a psych student from BCCC and I'm supposed to be observing in counseling today."

"Of course, dear. Do you have your authorization form?"

I exhale dramatically and let my shoulders sag hopelessly. "I wish. I went to the department office early this morning, but my professor was snowed in and couldn't meet me on campus. She called in the approval, but the secretary wouldn't give me the form. She's kind of a stickler, you know?" I let my eyes wander toward the principal's office and Donna Jo.

The sweet nurse smiles knowingly and nods. "Well, I'm sure everything is in order, and I know you have to get these things finished before the semester ends." She opens a three-ring binder and makes a few notes. "Write your name on this badge."

She slides an "Authorized Visitor" badge toward me and I'm in such a hurry to complete the transaction I start to write "M" instead of "D." Do you have any idea how hard it is to make that look like a ridiculous and on-purpose flourish? I peel off the sticker and press it onto my Donna Karan suit jacket.

She smiles and reaches for a clipboard.

Movement in the principal's office catches my eye. Donna Jo and Brynley are wrapping things up. I've got to giddyup!

"Sign here, dear."

I sign so fast that I'm honestly not sure which name I write. "Can you point me to the counselor's office?"

"If you wait a jiffy, I'm sure Brynley can escort you on her way to English."

Panic grips my chest. I feel more than certain that Donna Jo will not buy my cockamamie story. If

I don't high tail it out of here, my cover will be blown before the end of first period. "Oh, I'm so late already. I feel just awful. Can you just tell me where to turn?"

She shuffles around the counter as Donna Jo turns to leave the back office. I pivot my gaze and smile broadly at Mrs. Boulton.

The lovely woman slips an arm around my shoulders. "Don't fret, dear. Ms. Olson is very understanding. She'll give your professor a good report. Come along, I'll show you the way."

Donna Jo reaches the counter just as we pass through the doorway into the hall.

I refuse to look back. Never look back. Movie heist 101: once you've successfully passed the checkpoint, never look back. My pulse is racing and I feel sweat evaporating from my hairline. I take a deep breath.

Mrs. Boulton gives my shoulders a little squeeze before dropping her arm. "That's it. Just a few deep breaths and you'll be all set." She pauses and gestures to a closed door. "It looks like Ms. Olson forgot about your appointment, or maybe she got snowed in. She lives down a long dirt road out by Clear Lake. Well, I guess we better head back to the front office and see if Donna Jo can reschedule your visit."

My stomach is flipping like a gymnast in a floor

routine. "Maybe I could just shadow you today? I have to turn in this paper by Friday and my professor never gives extensions."

Her face wants to say "no," but my wonderful little gift of clairsentience *feels* that her heart wants to say "yes." I simply need to give her a reason. Done. "It's absolutely my fault that I waited until so late in the semester to schedule this. I was just so overwhelmed with caring for my grandmother . . . Now I'm going to flunk and I'll probably lose my scholarship." Is that a tear? Did my performance bring a tear to this woman's eye? Oh boy, now I feel sick to my stomach for a whole different reason. It's official: I'm a terrible person.

"Why, aren't you the sweetest thing? Of course you can shadow me. It's actually perfect timing since I have to give my health talk to all the junior and senior classes today."

I grasp her hand in both of mine and gush, "Oh, thank you. Thank you so much. You're a life saver."

After a brief stop in the teachers' lounge to get our coffee, Mrs. Boulton leads the way to her small, sterile office. Her desk is a half-size folding table with a chipped lamp, a notepad, and two pens. In the corner are two spartan, uncomfortable-looking cots covered with white sheets and equally white paper. A thin suggestion of a curtain hangs between the gurneys. Despite the fact that I hated school and have nothing but painful, lonely memories of my pre-matriculation days, I feel terrible about the obvious lack of funding at this institution.

"What can I do to help you prepare for the talks?"

"You don't actually have to do anything, dear. The Birch County Community College students usually just observe."

"Well, I'd like to start a new trend." I smile broadly. "Put me to work, Nurse Boulton."

"Well, alrighty. Boy, I love your attitude, Darcy."

"Oh, it's M—my pleasure." I barely caught myself before I blew my own cover. I have to get it through my thick skull: today I am Darcy. Darcy. Darcy. Darcy. I won't even think the other name. All Darcy. All day.

"Here's the key. You open that grey cabinet over there and get out ten condoms, the sample packet of birth control pills, and a big stack of the abstinence pamphlets."

My feet fail to move and my face is certainly near fire-engine red. I mean, what are the odds that I show up for my undercover routine on the very day of *THAT* health talk? I guess I'll have quite a story for Grams tonight.

"Don't worry, dear. I'll do all the talking."

I gulp audibly and collect our supplies.

The first two presentations are uneventful. A cheerleader named Traice asks an innocent question laden with double entendres, which incites uncontrollable snickering, and a young man named Khlab—pronounced cay-lebb; don't worry, I couldn't figure it out either—wants to know if minors are allowed to buy condoms. His question draws a few hoots from the jocks in the back row.

By the time we get to the junior class presentation right before lunch, I feel like an old pro. In fact, I recognize my office buddy, Brynley, sitting in the center of a group of orbiters. I remember this group of girls too well. Whatever the "sun" said, the "planets" would follow. Maybe my deep dislike of morning has something to do with my overt distaste of "suns."

She's tapping and scrolling on her phone as though her life depends on it, and the surrounding girls are glued to the screen.

Apparently, she got her phone back from the principal this morning. Her family is either wealthy or politically influential. In my experience, those kids can get away with anything.

Nurse Boulton calls the class to order and begins her presentation.

Since it's my third time through, I let my eyes wander up and down the rows of desks. Before my fashion training with Grams, I never would've noticed that Brynley's Marc Jacobs bag is a knockoff, or that one of the orbiters has colored in the scuff marks on her platforms with a Sharpie. A tickle at the edge of my consciousness picks up on a deviation from the speech.

"Oh, is that so, Stellen?" Brynley crosses her arms and smirks.

"It's a valid question." I assume the boy responding is Stellen.

"Not for a creepy little woodchuck stuffer like you!" Her eyes flash, and the "planets" all giggle maniacally.

The boy picks up his backpack and runs out of the room with his head down.

Mrs. Boulton calls, "Stellen. Stellen, you do not have a hall pass."

I put a hand on her arm. "I'll go after him. You finish your talk."

A murmur washes over the classroom. I nearly forgot what a hot piece of . . . property I am in almost-Canada. I put a little *extra* in my "shake" as I leave.

"Stellen?" I walk around the corner, based completely on the inexplicable feeling in my gut. Whimpering and sniffling confirm my hunch. "Stellen, do you want to talk about it?"

The young boy shakes his head of dark-brown curls and wipes the tears from his green eyes.

This guy is probably going to mature into a dangerously handsome twenty-something, but the crushing humiliation of high school is completely robbing him of embracing his potential.

"I'm fine. I'll just go to the principal's office and say I was wandering without a hall pass."

"You don't have to do that. We stepped out of class to discuss a private matter. You haven't broken any rules."

The genuine gratitude that pours out of his up-turned face nearly breaks my heart.

"For real?"

"For real. Brynley and her pack of hyenas can take a hike."

He chuckles and hiccups a little. "A stuffed hyena. Now that would be something to see."

I narrow my gaze and wonder how the word stuffed can appear in conversation twice in the space of two minutes. I worry that little Stellen might be some kind of psycho serial killer with plans to turn his enemies into trophies. "Stuffed hyena?"

"Oh, yeah. My dad's a taxidermist. That's why they all tease me about my freezer full of dead animals and call me a woodchuck stuffer."

I breathe a sigh of relief. "They used to call me *Powder*."

His whole face lights up. "Like the movie? I

love that film. I mean, my dad loves to skin animals and all that taxidermy stuff, but I want animals to live. I love that movie."

"Too bad we didn't go to high school together, Stellen. I think we would've been friends. You know?"

"Totally." He stares off into the distance. "I don't really have friends."

"Well, you have one now." I put out my hand.

He shakes it as he says, "Thanks, Miss Brown."

Oh crap. So much for giving this kid a little faith in humanity. Probably best to tell him the truth immediately. Rip the Band-Aid off. Right?

"There she is! That's her!"

The skin on the back of my neck prickles before I turn. Donna Jo is frantically waving her appendages at me, and the one and only—

"Miss Moon, I should've known."

As I watch Stellen's eyes fill with hurt and confusion, my usual elated tummy tingles are replaced with sudden nausea. "Hi, Erick."

"It's still Sheriff Harper, Moon." He pulls the cuffs from his belt. "You know the drill."

"Miss Brown, what's—"

I turn away from the betrayed teen and put my hands behind my back.

"Mitzy Moon, you are under arrest for possible child endangerment, false . . ."

The rest of Erick's speech is lost to me. I can't believe things ended up like this. I had no business coming to this school. What was I thinking? I've finally sunk as low as—

BRRRRRRRING!

Spoke too soon.

Doors burst open and the hallway fills with a swarm of loud, rushing students. It reminds me of a slot canyon during a flash flood back in Arizona. It's like white noise, but it can't drown out my shame.

Some students slow and stare at the sheriff and me in the handcuffs, a few pull out their phones and record the event, but most hurry past to their next class.

I search the swirling crowd for Stellen, but he's vanished into the sea of humanity like a pebble in a dry riverbed. However, my humiliation is far from over.

"Darcy, what on earth happened, dear?" Mrs. Boulton's friendly concern stabs into my heart like a knife.

"Long story. I'm really sorry." I can't make eye contact.

"Come on, Moon." Erick puts one hand on my shoulder and one on my cuffed wrists as he steers me, not unkindly, toward the exit.

Donna Jo follows, sputtering all the way. "This never would've happened if I'd been on the front desk. I can assure you that Principal Puig is going to hear about this. I've been saying that Boulton woman . . ."

The rest of her tirade is muffled as Erick places that movie-classic hand on my head as he puts me in the back of the patrol car and slams the door.

He slides into the driver's side, calls in to dispatch, and drives away from the scene with a half-wave, half-salute to Donna Jo.

"That was all for show, right? I mean, you're just going to drive me back to the bookshop and forget this ever happened."

Silence.

"I can explain, Erick."

Rather than a direct answer he depresses the button on his radio and says, "Dispatch, this is Sheriff Harper. Can you let Silas Willoughby know that we're bringing Miss Moon in on possible child endangerment charges?"

"10-4, Sheriff."

The emphasis he places on "Sheriff Harper" lets me know beyond a shadow of a doubt that I've crossed a line, perhaps *the* line, and this is one dust bunny I can't sweep under the rug.

CHAPTER 7

As SHERIFF HARPER marches me through the station, I feel worse than during any previous walks of shame in memory. The chipped paint on the metal desks and the warped paneling on the back wall fail to amuse.

The cold metal chair in Interrogation Room One feels harsher than I remember, and it's worth mentioning that Erick does not unlock my cuffs before he plants me in it.

"I'll be back once Willoughby shows."

He does not ask if I want coffee. He does not ask if I need a restroom. He does not smile. I really stepped in it this time.

I'm left to stew in my own juices for some time. I suspect Silas is also taking his sweet time in responding in an effort to teach me some additional lesson.

Lesson learned, all right? I know it was a bad idea—now. At the time, it seemed like a completely legitimate way to find the kid who owned the DC shoes. I can't put my finger on why I thought that was so important, but I did. I still do.

Despite the trouble I'm clearly in, I feel—and yes, I mean feel in the weird woo-woo way—in my gut that the shoe print is somehow connected to Ledo's accident. But I'm of no use to Doc Ledo if I'm sitting in the slammer, so I better spend this time coming up with the world's greatest reason for sneaking around a high school under a fake name.

By the time my underwhelming lawyer pushes open the door and joins me in the claustrophobic space, I'm wedged somewhere between relief and frustration. However, I think I might have the perfect cover story.

"Hey, Silas. Do you want to see me get out of these handcuffs?" The reference to one of my previous alchemy lessons fails to garner the desired response.

He does not reply. He scrapes back the chair on the opposite side of the table and heaves his tattered briefcase onto the flat surface as he drops toward the seat with a tortured exhale.

The unwelcome aroma of pipe smoke and denture cream wafts toward me, and Silas smooths his bushy grey mustache with disappointment and frustration.

"I have the perfect story."

He does not smile. He does not wink. He adjusts his brown bow tie and straightens his tweed coat. "These are very serious charges, Mizithra."

Uh oh. It's formal name time. Now I'm actually worried. "How serious?"

"False impersonation, conspiracy to commit criminal impersonation and second-degree conspiracy to commit harassment, disturbing school, possible child endangerment, and giving a false statement. Sheriff Harper informed me that the school district is threatening to push for felony false impersonation, due to the trauma caused to minors. You are facing up to three years in prison."

I don't handle bad news like most people. Ever since my mother was killed in a fatal car accident when I was eleven, I've had an intense aversion to accepting negative information. "Wanna see me get out of these cuffs?" I whisper.

"I would prefer if you would enlighten me as to the impetus of your visit to our local educational institution."

"It has something to do with Doc Ledo's accident."

A faint smile touches his mouth and his hound-dog cheeks quiver. "Would this pertain to 'something' you sensed?" A hint of the patient mentor within emerges.

I nod.

He smiles in earnest. "Go on."

"Ever since I read the article in the newspaper and saw the picture of the footprints in the snow, I haven't been able to get the image out of my mind. I know—deep in my gut—I know it has something to do with the hit and run."

"I see." He leans back and strokes his mustache. "Did you discover any additional information at the school?" Keen interest lights his milky-blue eyes.

I shrug as best I can while in the handcuffs. "About the only thing I discovered is that high school hasn't changed one bit since I went, and the mean girls still rule the world." I think back to the pathetic furnishings in the nurse's office. "Oh, and that the school is severely underfunded."

A large smile lifts his jowls, and Silas scrunches up his bulbous nose as he leans forward. "I can work with that."

"Huh?"

The handle on the door twists.

Silas whispers, "As difficult as it may be, let me advocate on your behalf."

I offer a begrudging, "All right."

Sheriff Erick enters and stands next to the table.

I look up into his blue-grey eyes and smile in spite of my predicament.

"I hope your lawyer has conveyed the seriousness of the charges, Miss Moon."

"Well, here's the thing, Erick. It seems—"

Silas clears his throat loudly and bangs his briefcase from the table to the floor.

I snap my mouth shut and try to apologize to him with my eyes.

"What my client is attempting to explain, Sheriff, is the reason for her entrepreneurial fact-finding mission."

I lean back and my wrist pinches against the back of my chair. Even though I'm in a little pain, I think I'm going to enjoy this.

"This better be good, Willoughby." Erick crosses his arms over his broad chest and I can't take my eyes off his slightly bulging biceps.

"I assure you, Sheriff Harper, my client had the best intentions. You see, the Duncan-Moon Foundation is eager to support positive development and community renovation in our fair city of Pin Cherry Harbor. Having been a product of the foster-care system, Miss Moon had the opportunity to visit many schools in her young life. One of the causes she wishes to champion is proper funding for arts and sciences in our schools. Her undercover visit to the school today was at the behest of the Foundation and was for the sole purpose of identifying the programs most in need of the Foundation's generosity." Silas punctuates his soliloquy with a meaningful head nod and a tamping of his mustache.

I'm so amazed by the yarn my lawyer has spun that I'm leaning forward, hanging on every word. However, Erick didn't fall off the turnip truck yesterday. He stares stolidly at my attorney, but addresses me.

"And what did you find, Miss Moon."

Thankfully, I too have been off the vegetable transport for some time. "I'd have to say that one of the programs most in need is student services. The nurse's office is sadly under supplied and the total lack of patient privacy has to be a violation."

Silas fixes me with a "quit while you're ahead" glare.

Erick's arms slowly uncross and he places both hands on the table as he leans deliciously close to me. "Moon, I don't know if you're this good or this bad, but I hope you have the cash to back up this ridiculous fairytale."

I'm so mesmerized by the proximity of Erick's full, pouty mouth that words have vanished from my brain. Luckily, Silas is unflappable.

"As soon as we complete our evaluation the Foundation will be cutting a check to the Birch County School District, earmarked for Pin Cherry Harbor High School, of course."

Erick stands and shakes his head. "Of course."

"Now, can you remove the restraints from our generous local philanthropist?" Silas smiles pleasantly.

The sheriff scoffs. "Stand up, Moon. Once again it would appear that this is your lucky day."

I silently follow orders and can't help but think that Silas has used his alchemy voodoo to glue my mouth shut, because however hard I try, I can't seem to release my inner snark.

The cuffs come off and I rub the red indentations on my wrists.

"Come along, Mitzy." Silas gathers up his briefcase and leads the way out of the interrogation room.

I take a step toward the door that Erick is holding open, but my right foot catches on the table leg—which is screwed to the floor—and I sail headlong into Erick's rock-hard chest.

He fumbles with the door, manages to catch me with one arm, but has to release the door to keep from losing his own balance. His left hand comes around to lift me back to standing and grazes my boob area, finally releasing my trapped tongue.

"That's the second time you've gone to second base with me, Erick, and still no dinner."

He turns as red as a pin cherry, and I let myself out of the room that seems to have shrunken to the size of a broom closet in the last few seconds.

CHAPTER 8

SILAS DROPS ME at the bookshop in his 1908 Model T, which I'm sure isn't winter-worthy, and informs me that he will have someone retrieve my Jeep after school hours and will contact the school board to see how sizable a donation will be required to erase my transgression.

I walk into the bookshop filled with visceral relief followed by a fit of giggles as I mumble, "We do more before 9:00 a.m. than most people do all day."

"Who does, honey?"

And we're back to Bladder Control 101! "Grams, we agreed on the slow sparkle re-entry. Remember?"

She chuckles. "Right! Sorry, dear."

I slip a belated hand over my mouth and glance around the bookstore. "Are we alone?"

"Not even close, doll," calls Twiggy from somewhere in the stacks. "But if you're asking if there's anyone here who doesn't already know that you talk to ghosts, that answer is 'no.'"

"Touché."

Twiggy and Grams both have a long chuckle at my expense.

"Oh well, I guess no one wants to hear about how I got arrested at high school and Silas had to invent a philanthropic organization to keep me from serving three years in prison."

I dust my hands together as though I'm finished with both of them and head toward the circular staircase.

Grams attempts to intercept me, but I walk through her phantasm—and straight into the immovable object: Twiggy.

"All right, Your Highness. Let's have the story." Twiggy walks to the back room as she calls, "I'll make tea."

I relent and regale the girls with my tale. Twiggy laughs at my misfortune until tears squirt from her eyes, while Grams swirls around the bookshop with a severe case of afterlife anxiety.

"Are you out on bail? Will there be a trial?" She spins upward.

I shrug and reply, "I believe the correct term is 'bribe.' I mean, Silas is going to make the school board an offer and just keep adding zeros until they say, 'Thank you for your donation' instead of 'Lock her up!'"

"After all of that and you still don't know whose shoes?" Twiggy snickers. "You're something else."

I exhale in a loud and offended way. "At least I was trying to follow up on my psychic clue."

Twiggy rolls her eyes. "So you say. Could you see the logo in the snow?"

"Yeah. It was from a pair of DC skateboard shoes. Like I said at the beginning of the story, that was why I went to the school."

"Oh, I got that part, doll. I was just thinkin' that if you could see the logo, then it wasn't covered by snow. I guess the statue musta been stolen right before the storm ended."

Grams freeze-frames and my jaw drops.

Twiggy winks at me. "I'll leave you to chew on that, and you can pour your own refills on tea. I gotta get home and feed the dogs."

"Reeeee-ow." A warning.

"Oh, take it easy, Pye." Twiggy bends and scratches his arched back. "See you three stooges tomorrow." And with one last piercing cackle, she's gone.

I whip out my phone and call Silas. "Hey, I— You're right, a proper greeting would be more civilized." I put on my poshest British accent. "Good evening, Mr. Willoughby. Would you be so kind as to inform me if you've obtained a copy of the police report?"

Grams shakes her head. "You shouldn't make fun, dear."

I point to the phone and nod. "I wasn't making fun."

Ghost-ma "tsks" several times and disapparates.

"Which police report?" I feel his mildly insulting insinuation is directed at me. "No, not mine. I actually meant the accident report from Doc Ledo's hit and run."

Grams reappears right in front of me and I gasp and jump back, nearly falling over Pyewacket.

"I'm fine, just dealing with a little interference on my end. Would you mind bringing the report over? I have an idea."

Pyewacket threads himself around my ankles in a suspiciously supportive manner.

"Yes, I am embracing my gifts . . . All right, we'll see you soon. Thanks."

By the time Silas arrives, I've polished off some leftover "hot dish" (a.k.a., casserole) from the fridge and let Pye out for his nightly prowl.

My alchemist-lawyer enters and, while I lock the front door behind him, he slips on his magicked wire-rimmed spectacles and searches the air. "Ah, Isadora. You look lovely, as always."

She waves and curtsies.

"So, how are you coming on figuring out a way to hear her?"

"My research continues." His face grows pensive.

I hastily change the subject. "Were you able to get the report?"

He hands me a folder and I flip it open. My eyes search through the messy handwriting of the officer on the scene. The ever-annoying Deputy Pauly Paulsen. To say that the woman despises me would be a severe understatement. Ever since I arrived in this town and wound up temporarily accused of murder, that woman has been out to make my life miserable. Hopefully, I can find what I need in this report and avoid having to get additional information directly from her pudgy little face.

"Ah ha!" I stab my finger onto the paper as though I've solved the Millennium Prize.

"What is it?" ask Silas and Grams in unison.

"The time of the accident."

Grams swirls her hands in the universal sign for "continue."

"It says that the snowplow operator found Ledo at 8:45 p.m. and his coat was covered by a fine layer of snow. There were no witnesses. Everyone was at the Extravaganza. It sure was lucky the plow went through that neighborhood when it did."

Silas harrumphs and strokes his grey mustache with his thumb and forefinger. "The plow always goes through The Pines first."

"What do you mean 'The Pines?'"

"What was the location of the accident? Precisely?"

I run my finger across the report. "Says here, the body was found on Pin Cherry Lane between Spruce Street and Fir Street."

"The Pines," repeats Silas in a tone that indicates he's answered my question.

Fortunately Grams floats in with much needed details. "The Pines is the upper-class end of Pin Cherry, dear. The wealthy retired folks, the doctors, judges, and moneyed widows all live in The Pines. The snowplow hits their neighborhood first, because if she doesn't the complaints will be the top story in the *Post*."

"She?"

"Artie. She's been running the plow since my fourth husband and I got back from our honeymoon."

I wave my hands to interrupt any further honeymoon-related information. "That's plenty for now. Let's get back to the accident report." I re-find the bit of data I was about to share before the "Artie" tangent. "Here it is. The actual time of the accident was calculated based on snow accumulation on the body and the known time that the snow-fall ended."

"Which is?" prompts Grams

"They say Ledo was struck at 8:25 p.m." I close the folder and look at Silas. "I need crime scene photos."

"That may prove difficult. May I ask why?"

"I need to compare the snow cover on the body with snow cover on that footprint . . ." Instinctively my eyes are pulled to the mood ring. The swirling black clouds shift to pure white and the footprint appears. My stomach clenches and my mouth goes dry.

"Mitzy?" Silas places a hand on my shoulder. "Are you all right?"

"He saw," I whisper.

"Ledo stated repeatedly that he never saw the vehicle." Silas squeezes my shoulder.

"No." The hollow gulp in my throat seems to echo off the tin-plated ceiling. "The thief. He saw the accident." And now I can't breathe.

CHAPTER 9

AFTER A LENGTHY PEP talk from my attorney followed by endless ghost-pats on my back from Grams, I manage to get some sleep, but the pale grey light of morning does not relieve the tightness in my chest.

All night long I struggled to make a decision. Part of me wants to run down to the sheriff's station and share my great lead, but the other part of me wonders how bonkers I'll sound when I state my source as "a feeling."

I need to talk to Artie and see if I can find something concrete to back up my psychic sensations.

"That really is the best idea you've had, dear."

I'm too exhausted to scold Grams for thought-dropping. "Did my whirring brain keep you up too?"

"I don't actually sleep, honey."

"Right. That does make more sense than what I was picturing." I can't keep the image of little ghost beds all filled with ghosts and each one tucked in with sheets, which may or may not be part of their floaty-ghost robes . . .

"RE-ow." Feed me.

Grams runs her fingers along Pye's arched back. "Sounds like you and Mr. Cuddlekins both need some breakfast."

I glance at the menacing form of Pyewacket slinking across the bed with devilish mischief in his eyes, and I tumble to the floor before he can pounce.

"Come on, Pye. Let's get me some wake-up juice." I press the plaster medallion above the intercom and my secret bookcase door slides open as Pye shoves past and races down the stairs. "Geez! Looks like someone's having a Fruity Puffs emergency."

"Oh, Mitzy, you crack me up." Grams snickers and vanishes into the floor.

I'm definitely up earlier than usual. I deduce this from the lack of coffee in the coffee pot and the absence of Twiggy's cackle when I trip over the— "Pippi Longstocking!"

Grams suppresses a chuckle.

"That book was not there when I walked in."

I narrow my gaze and size up potential suspects. Grams has recently acquired some limited abilities in the "affecting solid matter" department, but Pyewacket has a long history of torturing me with found objects.

Pye has finished his breakfast and sits innocently cleaning his whiskers and paying me no mind.

"Robin Pyewacket Goodfellow, did you do this?"

He pauses in his ablutions, and for a moment I feel as though he may speak.

He turns and saunters out in silence.

I exhale and retrieve some much-needed coffee from the barely filling pot.

Grams interrupts my java infusion. "I know you didn't ask out loud, but it wasn't me. I'm pretty sure it was there when you walked in, but you just missed it out of pure luck."

I plop unceremoniously into a stiff-backed wooden chair and rub my wounded toes. After two more glorious sips of go-go juice, I investigate the tome.

"STANDARD LEVEL BIOLOGY." I drop the book on the table and get a café au lait refill.

Grams floats toward the book and sighs.

"Nothing? No quip to explain this book's appearance?"

"I have no idea, dear. What would any of us want with an outdated high-school textbook?"

And there go the hairs on the back of my neck. "How do you know it's a high-school textbook?"

Grams waves her ring-ensconced hand toward the book.

As the coffee works its magic, I see the words stamped on, what I have come to learn is, the fore edge of the pages. "Property of Pin Cherry Harbor High School." I run my thumb across the words and smile. "I told you there was something I needed to know at that high school."

Grams whirs toward my face and places a fist on her hip while she wags a misty finger in my direction. "Don't you dare set foot in that school until Silas gets this mess sorted out. I will not last another one of my loved ones landing in jail."

And here come the tears. "Grams, please don't cry." I make an attempt to comfort her ethereal form.

"You need to go talk to Artie. You stay away from that school, and you interview her instead. Promise?"

"I promise, Grams. Am I allowed to grab breakfast at the diner before I track down this 'Artie' woman?"

"Of course, dear."

I pull out the haunches of my reindeer onesie and curtsy. "Why, thank you, ma'am."

After a quick-change that would make the cast of *Saturday Night Live* jealous, I hurry through the crisp air, snow crunching under my feet, toward the diner.

Let the record show, I never expected snow to crunch. I thought snow was always light and fluffy and silent. But I have a new appreciation for the Foley artists on those frozen-tundra *National Geographic* specials. The sound a polar bear makes as he crosses the Arctic is not a movie myth. That's straight up, authentic snow-crunch.

I pull open the door and nearly drool on my own chin when I smell the wondrous breakfasty yum that is Myrtle's. This glorious little touchstone in my daily routine is one of the many things that makes Pin Cherry feel more like home than anywhere else I've ever lived. I might even start to believe that I deserve to have a home.

Odell salutes me with his metal spatula and I take a seat at the counter so I can chat while I wait.

"I'll have the special."

"Already makin' it."

I nod. And that's what passes for "chat."

"Odell said you're looking into my brother's accident. Do you have any leads?"

I smile at Tally as she sets down my coffee, and

direct my answer to them both. "I'm talking to Artie today. I'll know more after that."

Tally's flame-red topknot bobs with fervor. "Bless that woman's heart. She saved Ledo's life."

I nod and smile. "Does Ledo live in The Pines?"

"Well now, technically I'd have to say 'no' because he lives on the opposite side of Pin Cherry Lane, you know? But he walks home from his clinic through The Pines every night, if you're wondering what he was doing."

Her tone is more defensive than I would've expected. "I'm sorry to bring it up, Tally. I only learned last night that The Pines is the first place to be plowed after a storm. I just thought it was fortunate—that's the wrong word." I take a long sip of my coffee before I say anything else stupidly inappropriate.

Tally scurries away to fill other, more deserving coffee cups.

Odell shakes his head. "Tell Artie I said 'hello' won't ya?" He brings out my plate and leans toward me as he slides it on the counter. "Tally's been on edge since the accident. I don't think she's ready to accept Ledo's prognosis."

He raps his knuckles on the counter and heads back to the kitchen.

I wolf down my food, finish my coffee, and yawn indelicately. "Where can I find Artie?"

"Down at the substation."

I lift my hands and nod encouragingly.

"You know where Final Destination is, dontcha?" He snickers.

I pretend not to receive his meaning. "If you're referring to the tavern located near the docks, I've heard of it."

Odell fails to hide his amusement. "Well, there's a city building across the street. Garage is in the back."

"Thanks."

I hurry back to my own garage and climb inside my frosty Jeep. I crank the nonexistent heat and cautiously reverse down the alley. The vacant building next to me has attracted some interest lately, and a couple of days ago I nearly backed over a realtor.

As the waterfront dive bar Final Destination looms into view, I swallow and shake my head. It started out as a fun place to play pool and ended up the site of a kidnapping. But that's another story, and today I need to stay focused on Artie and whatever information she might have.

I drive around to the back of the city maintenance building, and the huge metal rollup garage door is open. Shoot, I hope she's not out plowing the streets. Guess I didn't really think this through. I park partially wedged in a snowbank and run across the street into the substation. A massive dump truck with a plow on the front fills the space. "Artie? Artie? Odell says 'hello.'" A metal chair scrapes across the floor and something crinkles.

As I come around the front of the monstrous vehicle, a small woman with curly grey-brown hair and a thick plaid coat dusts off her hand on her dungarees as she walks toward me. "Hey there, I'm Artie. Don't mind the sour cream and onion dust. A girl's gotta eat."

I like her already. "Hey, Artie, I'm Mitzy." I extend my hand in the customary greeting and she nearly crushes my bones.

"How ya doin'? You said something about Odell? That old scoundrel! He still owes me fifteen dollars for a bet he lost in 1983."

"That sounds like Odell. He's—I mean he was—good friends with my grandmother. I'm looking into Doc Ledo's accident for Tally. I'm just trying to see if there's anything the authorities might've missed."

Artie slaps her hand on her thigh and reaches out to give me a second even more vigorous handshake.

"Well doesn't that just beat all! You're *that* Mitzy. I'm happy to help Doc Ledo in any way I can. Have a seat." She gestures to a paint-chipped perch that looks as cold as it does uninviting. "Have a seat and ask me anything you like."

I stare at the metal chair, barely thirty feet from the wide-open garage door, and can't hide my frown. I was hoping there would be an actual office somewhere, with a door and a heater.

But Artie takes no notice of my hesitation. She scrapes her chair back, sits down, and slides her bag of chips across the scarred tabletop. "Help yourself."

"Sure, thanks." I definitely don't want to offend her, so "when in Rome." I glance at the imposing truck and prompt, "So tell me about your plow."

Her face lights up like a Christmas tree and she launches into a lengthy explanation about horse-power, tandem axles, and several other attributes of her precious "beastie."

"Well, it's quite a machine." I glance up at the cab nearly ten feet in the air and chew the inside of my cheek. "The police report said Ledo's body was covered with a layer of snow. How did you even see him from up there?"

"When you've been doing this as long as I have, you learn how to tell the difference between a snowbank, a dead deer, and a man." Her tone has an edge, which I desperately need to soften.

"Of course, of course. I grew up in Arizona. I don't know the first thing about snow. I could really use a lesson from somebody with as much experience as you." Grams would be so proud of my "more flies with honey" approach. "When you saw how much snow had accumulated on the body, were you the one to point out to the sheriff how long Ledo had been lying in the street?"

"Boy, oh boy. The stories in the paper didn't exaggerate a thing. You really are a sharp cookie." She bangs her hand on the table for emphasis and retrieves her potato chips. Artie crunches through a handful before she answers my question. "I figure it couldn't have been more than twenty or thirty minutes from the time he was hit to the time I found him. The storm was slowing down, and the rate of accumulation had dropped by at least fifty percent since the peak of the storm—which I place at around 6:00 p.m. Once the worst had passed, I headed out and hit the main roads leading to the park—" She stops and looks at me with a warning in her eyes. "Now, don't go telling any of those hoity-toity Pines residents about my detour. I just wanted to make sure everyone could get to the Yuletide Extravaganza. Anyway, I headed over to The Pines by way of Gunnison and started plowing up and down their streets. Of course, Judge Carlson had to come out and flag me down so he could complain about me leaving windrows at the end of the driveways. I explained to him, for the two-hundredth time, that we don't have enough snowplows or operators to clean out resident's driveways, but after forty-some years on the bench, I guess he's earned the right to complain."

"Did you happen to see Ledo walking home from the clinic?"

"I certainly did not. I figure he'd already passed through The Pines by the time I got there, and I can't help kicking myself for coming in on the far side of the development. If I were to come in off Pin Cherry like I usually do, I might've seen who hit him. At least I would've gotten to him sooner; poor man was near frozen solid by the time the ambulance arrived. I called it in right away, set up flares, covered him with a couple of my space blankets. But I didn't dare move him, you know? I've seen enough TV shows to know not to move a body."

"I agree. Was there any debris around the body?"

"Well, the impact knocked him clean out of his winter boots. They were sittin' by the side of the street, but I didn't see anything else."

I shudder as I think about the amount of force it would take to knock a human being right out of their shoes. Poor Ledo. I absolutely have to figure out who did this to him. "Could you show me on a map or something exactly where you found the body?"

"Sure thing. Hold on." She scoots back her chair and heads to the ladder on the driver's side of the massive snowplow. She scurries up and swings into the cab in record time and returns with what looks like an iPad. She taps and swipes furiously before laying the screen on the table. "See this here, that's Spruce and this up here is Fir. Now, I was coming down Pin Cherry Lane and I saw the body in the road right here." She taps her finger on the screen twice and enlarges the image.

I nod my head. "And is there a driveway right here?"

She returns to her chair and shakes her head. "Not on that side of the street. There's the brick wall between Pin Cherry Lane and the houses in The Pines. All their driveways are inside the residential area. But the folks across the street on the other side of the Lane have driveways. This is probably about where 1872 Pin Cherry sits. But I don't recall any tracks comin' across the street. In fact, I don't remember any tracks on the other side of the body. It's almost like whoever hit him, backed away, turned and went the other direction. Unfortunately, my plow scraped up any tracks left in the street when I approached."

It all seems like a dead end. Her information confirms the time of the accident from the police report and that's about it. No new information. No amazing leads.

"Thanks for your time, Artie. I appreciate the

snowfall lesson and I'm glad to know you're the one running this beastie."

She chuckles with modesty as she gets up and grips my hand in another over-zealous handshake, while she pats me on the shoulder with her other large hand. "Any time. Absolutely any time."

I hurry back to my Jeep and wonder how I still have circulation in my fingers and toes. Maybe I'm growing accustomed to winter in almost-Canada. Or maybe my extremities are so numb I can't tell the difference.

CHAPTER 10

MY RETURN TO THE BELL, Book & Candle is far
less triumphant than I had hoped. I tug open the
intricately carved front door and bump directly into
a man backing toward the entrance.

"Can I help you?" I exhale the phrase with a
heapin' helping of snark.

"Ah, Miss Moon. My savior has arrived." Rory
Bombay slips an arm around my waist and gently
spins me between him and—

"Reeeee-ow." A warning.

I laugh in spite of Rory's desperately tense jaw.
"I see you've met our mascot, Pyewacket."

Pye responds with a "Ree-ow." Soft but condescending. Clearly he is not a fan of the term "mascot." I'm sure he would prefer "fearless leader" or
perhaps "god king." Spoiled little demon spawn.

"As much as I admire your intelligence, Miss Moon. I will be forced to emphatically disagree. That is a deadly predator, no high-school plushy."

"I'll settle him down." I walk toward Pyewacket as I admonish his poor manners. "Pye, Mr. Bombay is a guest. You will not eat our guests." I reach down to scratch his head between his lovely tufted ears and receive a sharp warning thwack from his right paw. I say "warning" in spite of the pain, because he did not extend the claws and claim a chunk of flesh.

Pye runs up the circular staircase before he can be properly scolded.

"Oh, that fiend!" I search the surrounding air for Grams. Oddly vacant. She normally swoops in to defend the little reprobate.

"Thank you for defending my honor, Miss—"

I spin around and wave my hands in surrender before he can finish that sentence. "Look, I've already got one eligible bachelor in this town stuck in the friend zone with this 'Miss Moon' nonsense. Please call me Mitzy." That sounded a great deal more flirt-forward than I intended. I hope he can't see the flush on my cheeks.

Rory's green eyes twinkle with amusement and his broad shoulders relax. "I'm flattered that you consider me eligible, Mitzy."

He nearly purrs my name, and I feel the heat from my cheeks turn into a tingle in my tummy.

Eager to change the subject, I ask, "Was Twiggy helping you to find something?"

He strokes his stubbled chin and shakes his head. "Not exactly."

"What do you mean?"

"I believe her precise words were, 'Get your grave-robbing hind end out of here.'"

I laugh much louder than is appropriate. "That sounds like her. What did you say to get on her bad side?"

"I was enquiring as to the possibility of gaining access to the Rare Books Loft."

"Did you make an appointment?"

He steps closer and lowers his voice to a husky whisper. "I was hoping for a private tour—today."

A fresh ripple of tingles washes over me, but it's quickly erased by a flash of icy warning from the mood ring on my left hand. I can't risk a peek, but I can sense with all my newbie psychic powers that something is not at all right.

Rory steps back and narrows his gaze. "Is every-thing all right, Mitzy?"

Something about the way he emphasizes "everything" sends another flash of warning through my aura. I'm just spitballing here, be-cause I don't know what to call the area around my body that is not my fleshy actual body. I re-member plenty of Sedona woo-woo folks using the word aura like it was a real thing, so I'm trying it out.

Rory takes another step back and straightens his wool coat. "Perhaps I've caught you on a busy day. Next time I'll make an appointment." He bows slightly and disappears out the door before I can reply.

"I thought he'd never leave!"

Adult diapers. This is my life now. I'm twenty-one years old and I'm going to have to start wearing adult diapers because my grandmother is a terror-ghost.

"I'm sorry, dear. But that man is bad news. You get Silas over here. He'll back me up."

"First, I'm going to change my pants, and then you can tell me all about how the road to Hell is paved with sexy, green-eyed men."

"For goodness' sake! At least give Silas a call before you go and change. Then he'll have a chance to get over here by the time you're ready." Grams swirls around me and puts on her very best sad-puppy-dog ghost-face.

I march to the back room and take a deep breath before I try my luck. "Twiggy, Grams caused me to have another accident. Would you mind calling Silas and asking him to come to the bookshop while I go put on some dry clothes."

Twiggy slowly rotates her captain's chair,

turning away from the computer screen and toward me. As her eyes take in what I'm sure is a hot mess, she replies. "Sure thing, Your Highness. Any additional mandates?"

"Not at this time." I head upstairs and leave Grams to haunt Twiggy into submission.

By the time I clamber back down the wrought-iron staircase in my "Never Trust Atoms, They Make Up Everything" T-shirt, Silas has arrived.

"Greetings, Mitzy. To what do I owe the pleasure of your invitation?"

"I'd like to discuss Ledo's case with you, but Grams has more pressing matters." She swirls over his left shoulder, and I see him shiver with the inevitable ghost chill that everyone but me seems to experience.

"Please continue."

"When I came back from interviewing Artie, Rory Bombay was here at the bookshop."

Silas turns and paces between the stacks. "I told you that man was trouble. He's far too interested in *Saducismus Triumphatus*. We may need to upgrade security at the bookshop. Both the physical and the alchemical."

"What's the big deal? So he's interested in reading some books. Is that a bad thing?"

Silas emerges from the stacks and fixes me with a truly intimidating glare. "Do you recall the story of how your grandmother and I discovered the means to tether her spirit to this bookshop so that she might have the opportunity to make your acquaintance after her death?"

Well, clearly I know the answer to this question. Is he testing me, or does he actually think that I never listen to him when he talks? "I actually do remember. Grams wanted to find some way to hang around and because she knew she was dying, she had time to plan for it. You helped her out by reading the books—"

"Precisely." Silas steeples his fingers and bounces his jowly chin as he waits for me to catch up.

"Oh. I see what you did there."

"I'm sure Twiggy can handle getting a physical security system installed. And I can handle the more—magical alarms." Silas moves to the bottom of the circular staircase and unhooks the chain. The "No Admittance" sign drops and he turns to look at me. "Perhaps you should accompany me. Much of this work is beyond your current skill level, but it never hurts to take advantage of an apprenticeship opportunity when one presents itself."

"Sweet! I'm in." The disappointed look in his eye and the ghostly "tsk" from my grandmother warns me too late that my overeager response is inappropriate.

He rethinks his route and steps off the stairs. "We shall start with the side door." Silas and his crumpled brown suit shuffle to the door that leads to the alley.

I fall into step beside him. "Can we talk about my thing now?"

"Certainly, Mitzy."

"So, I went to see Artie at the substation. She was the one who pointed out that the time of the accident could be calculated based on the amount of snow that had accumulated on Ledo's body as he lay in the road."

"Sounds like an intelligent woman."

"Sure. But it doesn't really help me. That information was already in the police report. I asked her if she saw anyone leaving the area, but she arrived long after the accident had happened."

"Driveways?"

I give myself a secret pat on the back before answering. "I asked that. All the driveways in The Pines apparently empty onto the side streets. And the driveways on the other side of Pin Cherry Lane didn't have any tire tracks that crossed the street. In fact, she said there were no tracks in the snow on the other side of the body. Almost like whoever hit him backed up, turned around and drove back the way they came."

"And where did she find the body?"

"She showed me on a map. It was between Spruce Street and Fir Street, just like the police report said. I asked her if she could be more specific and she said it was probably somewhere around 1872 Pin Cherry Lane."

Silas makes a little sound, which I'm not sure if I should identify as a gasp or a squeal. But in my experience Silas does not squeal.

He turns slowly and the look in his eyes is proud and kind. "Then you have your proof."

"Proof of what? Basically every bit of that information was in the police report. I had a weird feeling that whoever stole the angel statue saw the hit and run. But I didn't find out anything new. I didn't get any piece of information that confirms my weird claircognizant message."

Silas raises one thick grey eyebrow. "Didn't you?"

I rummage through the contents of the interview in my mind. It wasn't that long an interview, so it's not difficult to review the facts. "Well, about the only thing that I didn't know before I talked to Artie was the exact place where the body was found."

A smile grips the corner of his normally sagging mouth as he replies, "Indeed."

I glance down at the mood ring on my left hand and the broiling black storm clouds blow away to reveal that pristine footprint in the snow. "What's the address of the house where the robbery took place?" I ask.

"If memory serves, it was 1874 Pin Cherry Lane." His answer is equal parts smugness and satisfaction.

"I think I need to go see the sheriff."

Silas places a firm hand on my arm. "We must attend to matters here, before all else."

It's definitely not a request. An undeniable sense of compulsion floods through my body. However, I'm going to go ahead and convince myself that I've decided to stay of my own free will. "All right. Show me some magic."

Silas removes a marking pen from his inside coat pocket. "This is an ultraviolet marking pen. The symbols I will draw on the doors and window casings will not be visible to the naked eye. However, their power and influence will create the necessary barrier to any malevolent energy attempting to infiltrate the perimeter."

"Infiltrate? Perimeter? Are you like a wizard soldier now?"

"As we have discussed on more than one occasion, Mitzy, I am an alchemist not a wizard. And my concerns regarding the intentions of Mr. Rory Bombay are more than valid. Did your grandmother share any of his history?"

"His history? The man is barely ten years older than me. I doubt he could have much of a history with my grandmother."

Grams floats in with a hint of regret wrinkling her ethereal brow. "I hate to burst your bubble, dear. But that Rory scamp is older than he looks."

I suddenly don't think I want to hear this story.

"Well, whether you want to hear—"

I point to my lips and shake my head. "Lips did not move, Grams."

"Well, you're going to hear the story. It's for your own good." She preens her burgundy gown and begins, "My fourth husband was affectionately called a 'railroad tycoon.'"

I wave my hands to interrupt. "Wait, I thought your third husband was the railroad owner. I mean, didn't my grandpa Cal Duncan own the whole Midwest railway thingy?"

"Let's just say I have a type, honey. My fourth husband, Joe Willamet, was also in the railroad industry. However, he was Native American. I think it was—"

My attention drifts as I wonder if the end of marriage number three and the start of marriage number four, in such a socially adjacent position, have anything to do with each other."

"I'd like your full attention, Mizithra."

Uh oh, formal name time. I think I was definitely onto something.

Ghost-ma clears her throat loudly. "As I was saying, Silas represented me in my divorce from Cal, and we formed a friendship."

I smile at Silas. "Grams says you formed a friendship during her divorce from Cal."

Silas chimes in, "The friendship seemed to solidify *after* I secured her a more than generous settlement from Mr. Duncan."

"Would you two let me tell this story! Silas and I became friends, and as I started filling this bookshop with items that interested me, I began to build what is now the Rare Books Loft. Silas has always been a curious philosopher and he would spend hours paging through the magnificent tomes I'd collected, while I organized the day to day of the bookshop. Eventually, his knowledge of the arcane was as vast as any mortal could hope. He became adept at transmuting matter and other things. And, of course, you know how the story ends."

I could answer, but I feel like Grams just made the biggest jump-cut in movie history. One minute we're talking about someone reading a few books and the next minute that someone is creating a portal between this world and the afterlife—a portal where my grandmother can exist seemingly forever. "In the movie biz, we would say jump-cut to ghost of grandmother past."

Silas chuckles. "I wish I could hear her version. It sounds to me like she may have omitted the most torturous years of trial and error."

"I think you're right about that." Leave it to Silas to keep it real.

"Let's persevere with these protections. I don't believe it would be prudent to allow another night to pass without having taken every measure into consideration."

"Wait, that story didn't tell me anything about Rory."

Silas shakes his head. "Isadora, she has to know the truth. You can hardly expect her to heed our warnings on faith. Hereafter knows *you* never did." Silas wanders off to continue his emblazoning of symbols and Grams returns to finish the story.

"All right, dear. But I will expect to be given as much leniency as I've given you."

I open my mouth to protest, but memories of mumbling names in my sleep, bringing back questionable choices to the apartment, and my recent interaction with Mr. Bombay . . . I choose to nod my agreement instead.

"As my collection gained notoriety in occult circles, Mr. Bombay paid me a visit. He was extremely interested in several of the titles that I'd purchased and offered me exorbitant sums to take them off my hands. But I was more than comfortable, financially, and beyond that, there was something unsettling in his eyes. When I mentioned him to Silas, he decided to do some investigating."

"Silas? Investigating? So what you're saying is, I'm not the only one who likes to stick my nose where it doesn't belong."

A disembodied voice replies, "As a barrister, I have a duty to protect my client's best interests."

"Different words. Same meaning." I snicker.

Grams' ghostly chuckle fills me with a warm feeling of family happiness that I've missed more than I can say for the last ten years. "Please continue with your history lesson, Grams."

"Thank you, dear." She floats in front of the large six-by-six windows and continues her tale. "Silas suspected that Mr. Bombay was not his real name. Perhaps he had established an antiquities dealership under the pseudonym and traveled around the world collecting rare occult tomes and artifacts. Rumors of his collection ranged from fanciful to dangerous. Silas endeavored to test Mr. Bombay's intentions."

"That sounds like a risky plan." I tilt my head and narrow my gaze.

Grams emphatically nods her agreement. "We practiced the, for lack of a better word, 'spell' that would induce truth and then we invited Mr. Bombay to dinner. I set up an elaborate private

dinner in the Rare Books Loft. Of course, it was before I had purchased all the lovely desks paired with
those wonderful green-glass shaded lamps... Anyway, I had the loft decorated with beautiful lights to
create a magical setting."

"No pun intended, I'm sure."

"Oh, Mitzy, you're too much." Grams pushes a
shimmering hand in my direction. "As expected, he
accepted our invitation and arrived fashionably late
with a bottle of 1805 Terrantez Madeira. During
the course of dinner, Silas excused himself to open
the wine and used alchemical symbols to transmute
the liquid into the truth serum, like we had practiced. It was my job to keep Rory sufficiently distracted and entertained—"

I can't contain my overzealous chuckle. "Distracted and entertained? Is that what we're calling it
now?"

"Now, don't you start with me, young lady. I'm
a respectable woman of means, and I simply needed
information. I used the tools that were at my
disposal."

I gaze at the elegant apparition of my grandmother at her chosen ghost age of thirty-five and
smile. "You definitely were a hot number, Grams.
I'm guessing Mr. Bombay couldn't keep his hands
off you."

Once again a voice from offstage replies, "You

would indeed be correct, Mitzy." Followed by a deep, guttural chuckle from Silas.

"All right, you two, it feels like you're ganging up on me." Grams pitches a ghost snit.

"Grams thinks we're ganging up on her, Silas. I guess we best behave or I'll never get to hear the rest of story."

"Understood." Followed by a low chuckle.

"Please continue, Grams. I promise no further interruptions."

"Silas returned with the wine and my sparkling cider, and handed us each a glass. Somehow, Mr. Bombay saw through our ruse and switched his glass without us even noticing. Silas ended up drinking the truth-spelled wine and told him everything."

My eyes widen and I shake my head. "To quote Velma, 'Jinkies!'"

"I don't know who that is, dear."

"Not important. Continue."

"As you might've guessed, Mr. Bombay was furious with us and promised he would return with an offer we couldn't refuse. His tone was not friendly."

The ominous threat does not escape my attention. The Mr. Bombay that I met seems flirtatious, but ultimately harmless. And there's still the matter of his youthful appearance. "Okay, Grams, I get that you and Silas had dealings with someone named Mr. Bombay. But how can this possibly be the same guy? Are you sure this isn't a son, or possibly even a grandson of the guy you met?"

Silas shuffles in from wherever he had been marking his symbols and harrumphs loudly. "The information contained in these valuable resources"—he gestures to the books in my shop —"can be used for positive or negative results. Perhaps even a fountain of youth, as well as knowledge. And, to be fair, actions are subjectively interpreted. What some view as positive, others may view in a negative light. Take your grandmother, for instance. Trapping her spirit here in the bookshop so that she could partake of the opportunity to meet a long-lost granddaughter seems wholly positive. However, there are those who would say we have no business tampering with things beyond the veil. And perhaps they are correct."

Grams swirls down in a ghostly fury. "Don't you dare impugn my decision, Silas Willoughby. You are as much, if not more, to blame. Look at all the good we've done for Mitzy. Why, if we hadn't been here when she discovered her abilities... Who knows what might've happened."

Silence.

"Mitzy, tell him what I said. Tell him!"

I do as I'm told.

"My dear Isadora, I wholeheartedly endorse our

decision. I was simply demonstrating the effect of perspective for your dear granddaughter."

I step between my attorney and my Ghost-ma. "No fighting. I don't want to stand here playing the spirit version of 'Telephone!' Let's say I take your side and agree that Rory is trouble. How do I combat his obvious powers and knowledge? I have some gifts that I don't really understand, a dodgy ring, and a giant store full of books I've never opened! That hardly reads like the résumé of someone who saves the day."

Silas adjusts his faded bowtie and smiles. "Fortunately, you will most likely not be called upon to save the day. The protections I've put in place will discourage Mr. Bombay from returning and should also transmute his intentions should he cross any of these thresholds and enter your space. Your grandmother and I shall worry about Mr. Bombay, while you attend to tracking down this angel thief."

I'd actually completely forgotten about Dr. Ledo and the proof that confirms the clairvoyant, or clairsentient, message I received. "Right. Let me head over to call on Erick and see if I can stir up information, rather than trouble."

Grams chuckles openly while Silas has the decency to at least put a hand over his mouth.

"I'll see you two later."

CHAPTER 11

THE SHERIFF'S station is nearly deserted and the sullen officer minding the front desk is glued to her phone as usual. Maybe it's time to try a new approach. "So, what level are you?"

She hesitates, but she does actually flip her gaze from the screen of her phone and look at me.

Will wonders never cease? "I was asking what level you're at on Furious Monkeys?"

"Oh, I'm Level 83. This Furious Monkeys is just the best game ever! I so love this game. I don't know how I could make it through a shift in this boring, nothing-ever-happens station without this game. It's a lifesaver. No joke."

The flash of social energy shocks me into silence. I nod and smile.

"Are you here to see Sheriff Harper?"

I manage a brief reply. "Mmhmm."

Her eyes drift back to her screen and she gestures toward the sheriff's office.

I push my way through the swinging wooden gate and walk past the lonely metal desks in their crooked rows, with their messy stacks of paper and random coffee stains. In the student film I'm now making in my mind, this is a dolly shot and there's plenty of doughnut crumbs on the desks as well.

"Hey, Moon, can I help you?"

Oops, got lost in my mind movies again. But I'm pretty sure he didn't call me "Miss." Progress. "Hey, Erick, any leads on Doc Ledo's case?"

Erick's full lips smirk and he shakes his head, already defeated. "You know the speech. And I already gave your lawyer a copy of the police report."

I nod with more understanding than I've ever possessed. "Right. So, I'm sure you already made the connection."

The look on his face gives me all the answers I need. That's the wonderful thing about being an honest, upstanding, and unnecessarily sexy sheriff. Your face always tells the true story. "You should never play poker, Erick."

He chuckles and gestures for me to come into his office.

I let my face display an innocent gratitude, but my strut says "winner winner chicken dinner."

"So what's the connection, Moon?"

"The witness, of course." I really want to drag this meeting out as long as possible. And I only have one tiny piece of information, so I'm going to make it last.

"Witness? There were no witnesses. That's why the investigation has stalled out."

"Then my visit is definitely going to be the best thing that's happened to you all day." I'm not quite brave enough to wink, but I hope my smile conveys the message, "I'm the best thing that's going to happen to you, ever." I wait impatiently for him to beg.

"Is that so?" He leans back in his chair and laces his fingers behind his head.

Like one of Pavlov's dogs, I can't help but glance down toward his belt to see if possibly the corner of his shirt untucks and I can finally get a peek at what I know are absolutely washboard abs.

He clears his throat in a way that makes me feel like I'm not the only one with extrasensory perceptions.

"Right. Based on my investigation, there actually was one eyewitness to the hit and run."

He leans forward on his desk, and as his hands brush past his head a few strands of his gorgeous blonde hair knock loose and hang enticingly over his blue-grey eyes. Boy, this man knows how to derail an interrogation.

"How long are you gonna string me out? What did your investigation uncover?" He smiles in what I'm sure he meant to be innocence, but it's all kinds of enticing to me.

I don't particularly like the tone he used as he said "investigation." I think it's worth mentioning that my investigation has already uncovered far more than his. But I'm not here to play a comparison game. I'm here to get information. "Have you solved the case of the stolen statue?"

He chuckles. "This is starting to sound a little Agatha Christie."

I smile. "So you read detective novels? Does that improve your investigation skills?" I hope he picks up on my ironic tone.

He exhales and leans back.

Shoot. I pushed too hard, like always, and I lost my advantage.

"All right, Miss Moon. I do have an entire town to protect, so unless you have some additional information, I'll need to get on with my day."

When will I learn? "I thought it would be worth mentioning that whoever stole the statue saw the accident."

A little sparkle returns to his eyes and he leans toward me. "I'm listening."

"If you look at where Doc Ledo's body was found, the estimated time of the accident, and the footprints left at the scene by the angel thief, I think you'll see what I'm getting at."

His eyes darken. "Everyone was at the Yuletide Extravaganza. No one saw the robbery either. I can't imagine we'll have any more luck tracking down the angel thief than we did the hit-and-run driver."

Let the record show that I'm very pleased he's using my term "angel thief," and I guess I have to give him just a little bit more. "Well, I'm sure you noticed the footprint at the robbery was left by a DC skateboard shoe."

A smile, not of amusement, but of something more diabolical, spreads across Erick's face. "And now it would seem I've solved a different mystery."

I attempt to hold my features in their portrait of false innocence. "I'm not sure what you mean."

He stands and I struggle to keep my focus. "I think I just figured out what you were doing at the high school. And I'm pretty sure it didn't have anything to do with philanthropic evaluations." He walks around his desk and offers me his hand. I instantly take it without considering the implication. He pulls me firmly to my feet and leans down. "The school board dropped the charges, but I'm sure I could track down a parent or two who would be happy to pick up the ball and run with it. I suggest you get yourself out of my office before I have time to pick up that phone."

I yank my hand from his and scoot past him toward the door. I would like to point out that this takes every ounce of personal willpower I possess, because I would much prefer to have tripped and fallen all over him. "I hope you'll let me know if you turn up the suspect in the robbery, Erick. It was great chatting with you." I hurry out of the station so quickly, I forget to put a little extra wiggle in my waddle.

CHAPTER 12

As I PULL my hood up against the frost-laden air blowing across the now-frozen great lake, I catch sight of the sign above Myrtle's Diner. For the first time in recent memory, I actually can't remember the last time I ate. It certainly was today, wasn't it? I better go in and have some french fries just to be on the safe side. I push open the door and hurry into the welcome heat and delicious smells that await.

Red-vinyl bench seats all stand empty and only one man sits at the counter. Of course, if we all take a moment to remember my incredible luck with men, I'm sure you can guess exactly who's sitting at the counter. Let's say it together: Rory Bombay.

"Miss Moon." He rises from his stool and smiles that glorious, flirtatious, irresistible grin. He strides toward me and extends his right hand.

For some reason, I choose to play nice and extend my hand in return.

He grasps my fingers gently and brings the back of my hand to his lips. The subtle caress of his soft lips juxtaposing the roughness of his stubbled chin is exactly as delicious as I imagined that night at the Yuletide Extravaganza.

"Mitzy, I do hope you will forgive my ill manners at the bookshop. I've always been just a little frightened of cats. You see, my great-grandmother lost a child to a large black cat that was busily lapping dried milk from the child's face and inadvertently sucked away the infant's breath."

Now, I may not have lived through the depression, but I know an old wives' tale when I hear one. And this little anecdote couldn't be less true. In fact, I'm so sure that it is a falsehood that I don't even need to look at my mood ring for verification. However, as soon as the thought enters my mind, I can't resist a quick peek. Just as my eyes dart left, Rory drops my right hand and scoops up the ring-ensconced extremity.

"That is quite a fetching ring. May I ask where you got it?"

"I'd rather you didn't." The little hairs on the back of my neck pick up on a distinct shift in Rory's energy.

He covers as best he can. "Of course. All women must have their secrets."

I notice he doesn't release my fingers. I have no intention of causing further social tension by yanking my hand away, but I really don't want him staring at my ring. Thank heaven for small favors.

"This ain't a Sadie Hawkins dance. Did you come to eat or not, Mitzy?"

"I'll have the usual, Odell."

Rory regretfully drops my hand and invites me to join him at the counter. I feel powerless to refuse. And as I take a seat on the stool next to him, I suddenly wonder if the powerlessness is imagined or if it's caused by something Rory did. I have to shove all of this nonsense out of my head. Mr. Bombay has always been nothing but a gentleman to me, and Grams and Silas filled my head with a load of codswallop that I can't seem to shake.

Rory flourishes his hand near my right ear and produces a shiny copper penny. "A penny for your thoughts, Miss Moon."

Game on. "How old are you?"

He does not lean away. His green eyes sparkle with what I hope is only mischief as he replies, "I do admire your direct approach to life."

"That wasn't exactly an answer."

He lays the penny on the counter, leans back, and takes a deep breath. "I am older than I look.

Perhaps too old to be flirting with a lovely young woman such as yourself. But I've never felt that age should be a barrier or condition to truly exploring the possibilities of getting to know someone."

Now, how am I supposed to argue with that sentiment? If I insist on an answer, I'm going to appear shallow and unadventurous. Either he is sincere, or he is devilishly good at manipulating women. For now, I'm going to put all my eggs in the sincerity basket. "All right, I withdraw my question. But you only get one 'pass' and you've used it up. So you're going to have to answer this next question."

"Fair play to you, Miss Moon."

"Mitzy will be fine. And what I'd like to know is: What is your interest in me and my bookshop?"

"I believe that is actually two questions. Which one would you like me to answer today?"

Oh boy, he is good. "For today, I'd like to understand your interest in me."

"Very well. I find you fascinating. It's a small town and I've heard the rumors. And yet I see you walk through this city with your head held high. You seem to be adjusting well to your new life and your new standing in the community. In fact, I recently heard a rumor that you made a very large donation to the local high school."

As I open my mouth to protest, I see the corner

of his lip twitch as he struggles to keep his strong jaw from quivering with laughter.

I shake my head. I know when I've been beat. "Boy, there are no secrets in Pin Cherry Harbor."

Odell slides my plate in front of me with one hand and refills Rory's coffee cup with the other. "About the only secret that I can think of is what your dad is doing with his fine-looking lawyer down in Chicago."

Despite the wonderfully enticing man sitting next to me, my attention snaps to the curmudgeon serving my burger and fries. "What on earth are you talking about, Odell?"

He shrugs. "Jacob and Amaryllis came in here for breakfast three or four mornings ago and told me they were headed down to Chicago for a big train conference. Sounds like your dad planned to pursue a couple of new contracts and needed some legal advice."

I size up Odell for a moment while I formulate my follow-up question. "So what's the secret?"

"It's not my place to say, but I don't often get business associates sittin' on the same side of the booth when there's only two of 'em." He raps his knuckles on the silver-flecked white Formica counter and saunters back into the kitchen.

So many questions whirring through my head. But the biggest one is, obviously, why didn't my dad tell me he had a girlfriend? I mean, before my mom passed away, I used to fantasize constantly that he would return and they would get together and we would have a family. But I've learned a lot of things about my past that I didn't know before I came to Pin Cherry Harbor, and now the only thing I want is for my dad to be happy.

"If you'll pardon the interruption, I may have some information pertinent to your current dilemma."

"You know something about my dad's business trip?"

"I do not. However, I do know Amaryllis, and she is a lovely intelligent woman who, I would venture to say, has your father's best interests at heart."

Geez, this guy knows how to win a girl over. Whatever reservations I had when I walked through the front door of the diner and saw him sitting at the counter have all but evaporated. He's handsome. He's single. And he finds me fascinating. Silas and Grams are going to have to do a lot better if they want to discourage me from getting to know Rory. A lot better.

Rory drinks his coffee and finishes up the last of his pin cherry pie while I power through my burger and fried pieces of potato perfection. As I lick the salt from my fingers, Rory chuckles.

"I believe my instincts were correct. I thought it

best not to interrupt you while you were eating." He smiles and gives me a very yummy wink.

"It's been nice getting to know you a little better, Rory." I wipe my mouth with a thin paper napkin. "I have some leads I need to follow up, but I hope we bump into each other again."

"I would be delighted, Mitzy." He raises his coffee cup in a toast as I leave the diner, with a wave to Odell and a nod to Rory.

I decide to drive the few blocks over to Pin Cherry Lane, rather than risk potential frostbite walking in these icy, windblown conditions. As I pull into the driveway at 1874 Pin Cherry Lane, I realize I have no plan. But I seem to do my best work on the fly, so here goes. I make my way down the freshly shoveled and salted sidewalk and knock firmly but not threateningly on the front door.

The door opens almost instantly and a frail, white-haired woman standing somewhere between four and five feet tall smiles up at me as her cataract-laden eyes struggle to focus. "Good afternoon, dear. If you're looking for Brynley, dear, she left about an hour ago. Would you like me to get her cellular telephone number for you?"

Oooh, all my psychic senses are buzzing. Footprints in the snow. DC skateboard shoes. Kids in high school have them. This woman has a granddaughter in high school. Brynley—queen of the mean girls. I'm starting to feel rather confident that this theft had very little to do with the actual owner of the statue. "Oh that's okay, I have her number."

"All right then, dear. Who shall I tell her was calling?"

All the psychic powers I have, and I can't get my claircognizance to deliver a name! Come on, regular brain, it's in there somewhere! "Oh, tell her Sadie stopped by." I turn and jog back down the sidewalk before she can ask any additional mind-boggling questions. I hop in my Jeep and back out of the driveway, hoping against hope that Sadie is at least clique-adjacent.

I race back to the bookshop, taking unnecessary risks on the slippery streets and putting my limited winter driving experience to the test. Thankfully, when I get back to Bell, Book & Candle, Silas is tucked into a corner of the Rare Books Loft reading a thick leather-bound book trimmed by gilt edges.

"Ah, Mitzy. Any luck bamboozling the sheriff?"

Grams surges through the hidden bookcase door and floats eagerly beside Silas.

"I'll have you know that I handled myself very professionally and I already have an additional lead."

"What did I tell you about using the tools at your disposal?" Grams giggles like a schoolgirl.

"For your information, I actually went to the

house where the robbery occurred. In other words, I did my own legwork."

Silas carefully closes his book, slides back his chair, and shuffles over to the vacancy on the bookshelf where he replaces his reading material.

I'm extremely disappointed that no one is begging for additional information, so I launch into a voluntary account of my discussion with Brynley's grandmother and my confirmation that the angel thief was positively a high-school student.

"I'm glad to hear your instincts were on track."

"That's it? Are you not amazed?" I look from Ghost-ma to Silas and back.

"Oh, that's wonderful, dear."

"Well, if anyone has any great ideas . . . I need to get back into that high school. I know for a fact that the angel thief is there and I need to find the only eyewitness to the hit and run. I'm taking all suggestions. No idea will be ignored."

Grams slowly swirls up toward the ceiling and offers no brilliant strategies.

Silas strokes his bushy grey mustache with his thumb and forefinger, and unless my ears deceive me he seems to be humming under his breath. I pace toward the circular staircase and am nearly bowled over by a tan fur ball rocketing up the stairs. I jump to the side, and Pyewacket drops something before he races off down the left arm of the Ushaped mezzanine, his back end running catty-wampus to the front. I stoop to pick up his leavings.

"It looks like Pyewacket has figured out how to spend my money." I chuckle and walk toward the nearest trash bin.

"Perhaps you can delay for a moment, Mitzy." Silas gestures to the slip of paper in my hand.

I fan it back and forth. "It's a blank check. With claw marks in it. Apparently, he tore it out of the business checkbook. I'm gonna throw it away."

Silas puts a hand on his slightly round belly and laughs loudly. "Robin Pyewacket Goodfellow, you are a gentleman and a scholar."

I scrunch up my face and stare at my attorney. Is this what dementia looks like, I wonder? "Are you planning on letting me in on the joke?"

"You were looking for a way back into the school. I believe there's no better avenue than to present the principal with your donation in person. In fact, allow me to procure one of those oversized checks that sweepstakes companies are so eager to disperse, and I will see if the principal can organize an assembly for the presentation."

I stare at the blank check in my hand as a wave of goosebumps flutter across my skin from head to toe. That cat is far too human for my comfort.

CHAPTER 13

As it turns out, it's not that difficult to give money to high schools. Silas was able to organize a school-wide assembly in less than forty-eight hours. However, the rush-printing of the giant check proved to be a more monumental task. It cost a small fortune and had to be delivered by courier from Broken Rock. With all the pieces in place and the perfect subdued pantsuit with silk blouse selected by Grams, Silas and I load the giant check in the back of my Jeep and drive to the school.

Despite the secret being out that I am no longer Birch County Community College student Darcy Brown, but, rather, wealthy philanthropist Mitzy Moon, I enter the Pin Cherry Harbor High School gymnasium with more than my fair share of dread.

The bleachers are packed with students, teachers, and—something Silas forgot to tell me—parents. Wow! If I had any prior misgivings about public speaking, I suppose there's nothing like a trial by fire to cleanse them from my system.

Principal Puig stands atop a portable dais, behind a well-worn wooden podium, and speaks into a crackling microphone with the exact amount of feedback that you're expecting. If I were directing this student film, I would definitely instruct the camera operator to slow-pan the crowd and whip-pan to the principal.

"I'm sure you were all more than happy to hear that your second period classes would be canceled in favor of an impromptu assembly." Cheers and hoots emanate from the mass of hormones gathered on the wooden bleachers. "I am pleased to announce that our science program will be receiving a donation designated for new lab equipment, new textbooks, as well as a scholarship available for students pursuing bachelors of sciences after graduation." A smattering of applause from parents and a standing ovation from whom I'm assuming is the science teacher. "In addition, the English department will be receiving a sizable donation earmarked for the purchase of tablets to be used in the classroom, as well as a fund specifically for the library to purchase e-books which can be borrowed and read on the tablets."

This news receives larger applause than I would've thought. But I secretly worry that it's mostly for the tablets and very little for the e-books.

"And finally, a portion of this sizable donation has been set aside to fund a scholarship for a student pursuing an education in the veterinary sciences or veterinary medicine."

I smile and nod to the two people clapping.

"Students, faculty, and parents of Pin Cherry Harbor High School, please help me welcome our generous benefactor, Ms. Mizithra Moon."

Thunderous applause and feet stamping the bleachers assaults my senses. But beneath the din, I can still identify the subtle chuckling of Silas Willoughby. I'm sure he's quite pleased with himself. "Mizithra" is absolutely his doing. I do my best to strut across the shiny, highly polished gymnasium floor without slipping and making the wrong kind of spectacle of myself. As I approach the platform, the principal turns and offers me a hand. I'd like to ignore it and step up on my own like the empowered woman of means that I am, but the very real fear of my innate clumsiness choosing this moment to surface causes me to grab his hand in a near panic.

I manage to get myself on stage without any undue embarrassment and turn to retrieve the giant check from Silas.

Principal Puig returns to the microphone to announce, "Let's give another round of applause to Ms. Moon and the Duncan-Moon Philanthropic Foundation."

Another round of deafening applause answers the call as my eyes search the bleachers for Stellen. The cover story might be that I came to present a check, but in my heart, I'm willing to endure all the pomp and ceremony just to get a chance to apologize to that poor kid. Once again my attention wanders, and that seems like possibly the second or third time Puig had to repeat my name.

"Ms. Moon, did you want to say something?"

"Of course." I have no idea what I'm going to say, and playing dosey-doe with the principal while I'm holding a giant check and trying to get to the microphone proves difficult. Finally, he moves left when I move right, and I make my way to the mic, giant check in tow. "Good morning, everyone."

A general mumbling of something sounding a little bit like "good morning" follows.

Inspiration strikes in the nick of time. "I was here a few days ago on a research assignment from the Foundation and I had the pleasure of meeting several of you. My apologies for the secrecy surrounding my visit, but the Foundation felt it was important to get a realistic and unrehearsed picture of the programs at the high school. And I'm happy to say we found some great ways to help out."

Teachers and parents clap briefly.

I wonder if I'm allowed to do this, but I figure I'm the one holding the big check, so I can pretty much say whatever I want. "One thing Principal Puig forgot to mention, the Foundation has also designated a portion of the funds to remodel the nurse's office. We plan to build private exam rooms, a reception desk, and permanent storage cabinets." When I see the lone figure of Nurse Boulton stand to clap, I struggle to blink back tears. I don't know what makes that woman want to think the best of someone she barely knows, but I truly appreciate the vote of confidence. "Well, let's get on with this presentation. And if anyone has any questions for me, I'll be over there under that net hoop." I gesture toward the basketball hoop. Uproarious laughter and a few catcalls from the jocks echo through the gymnasium, but I know that a little self-deprecation goes a long way with this crowd. I step to the left and Principal Puig walks up to stand beside me. I maneuver the massive piece of laminated foamcore into position for the photo op and smile at Quince as he snaps away with his camera for the local paper. Heck, he probably takes pictures for the school paper too. We continue smiling for an uncomfortable amount of time and throw in several obligatory handshakes. As the applause dies down, Principal Puig takes the check and steps to the microphone. "All right. Everyone back to class. You will return to your second hour classrooms and your teachers will take roll. Do not attempt to skip out on the last ten minutes of your second hour. Detention will be given to anyone who does not report for this attendance." Principal Puig turns away from the microphone to address me privately. "Ms. Moon, I wanted to personally thank you for your generosity to our school. Educational funding is always a struggle and we certainly appreciate local benefactors putting the school at the top of their list. If there's ever anything I or Pin Cherry Harbor High School can do for you, please don't hesitate to ask." Another hearty handshake follows.

"Thank you, Principal. One thing you can do: please call me Mitzy."

"Of course. Of course." More handshakes.

"And if it's not too much trouble, could I possibly have a moment to speak with Stellen before he heads back to his second-period class?"

"Stellen? Stellen Jablonski?"

I'd really like to ask him how many Stellens go to this high school, but maybe it's a very popular name in almost-Canada. And I can nearly hear Grams whispering over my shoulder, "more flies with honey." "If that's the Stellen whose father is a taxidermist, then yes."

Principal Puig turns around and grabs the microphone. "Stellen Jablonski, please come to the platform before you return to class."

My eyes search the thinning sea of humanity and I locate the lone fish now swimming upstream. For some reason, tears well up in my eyes and I have to get a hold of myself. I twist my mood ring on my left hand and look up at the ceiling, while I blink back the emotion.

As the boy approaches, Principal Puig points to him and excuses himself to return to school business. I step off the platform and walk toward Stellen.

He stops, looks down at his feet, and stammers, "Hi, Miss Brown, I mean, Miss Moon."

"Hi, Stellen. I was hoping you would give me another chance?"

He pulls his eyes up from the floor and stares at me. "What do you mean?"

"The other day, when we were talking in the hallway, I meant what I said. I am your friend."

He looks up at me, shakes his head and shrugs. "It's okay. I know you were just doing the research for the donation or whatever. I've got friends."

I scan the empty gymnasium for a single straggler and see none. I'm all too familiar with putting on a brave face. In the foster system, I attended a new school almost every year . . . Sometimes two different schools in the same year. There was never anyone waiting for me either. "Yeah, I get it. I was just thinking that you mentioned you like animals. And I thought you might want to stop by my bookstore sometime and see my pet caracal." It's impossible to describe the instant transformation that takes place before my eyes. Stellen's spine gains strength, his shoulders square, and his face seems to glow from within.

"For real? You have a caracal? For real?"

I chuckle and nod. "He's quite a handful and he's addicted to Fruity Puffs, but I think he'd like you."

"That's lit! I have to get some stuff at Rex's after school tomorrow. Can I stop by then?"

"Sure. As long as you have your parents' permission." I don't really know if that's a thing, but I sort of feel like I shouldn't be inviting kids to my bookshop without their parents' buy in.

"Oh. I kind of don't want to tell my dad."

"Maybe you can ask your mom?"

"Um, well, the thing is . . ."

I'd recognize that hesitation anywhere. "Hey, it's cool. My mom died when I was eleven, so, you know?"

Stellen looks up as relief spreads across his face.

"Yeah, thanks."

"You don't think your dad will let you come to the bookshop?"

"Yeah, he'll let me. I just don't want him to know you have a caracal. I mean, like, he'd just want to stuff it. You know?"

I laugh in spite of the seriousness of the accusation that his taxidermist father would target my cat. "Well, Pyewacket seems to have far more than nine lives, so I'm afraid it will be a while before he's available for stuffing."

Stellen snickers and breathes a sigh of relief. "See ya tomorrow." He turns and runs out of the gym.

I feel pretty good about myself right now.

"That was a very kind thing you did, Mitzy."

And now a little squeak escapes my throat. I had completely forgotten Silas was waiting for me. "Boy, you and Grams just never get tired of scaring the bejeezus out of me."

Silas chuckles. "Come along, Mizithra. Let's get you back to the bookstore before you make any more expensive mistakes at this high school."

I follow Silas out of the gym and do my best to ignore the subtle shaking of his shoulders as he continues to be amused at my expense. All in all, this was the best day I've ever had in high school—hands down.

CHAPTER 14

As Silas and I head back to the bookshop, I attempt to reset my expectations to their normally low level. After losing my mother at such a young age and struggling through the foster system for more than six years, I tend to have a general suspicion of positive emotions. It's not that I don't enjoy being happy. Who wouldn't? It's just that in my experience the higher you let yourself climb the farther you end up falling. However, in spite of my internal red flags, I'm actually feeling pretty good about myself. I'm feeling confident in my choices.

I park the Jeep in the garage, and Silas and I walk down the alley. That is, until the heavy metal door of the building next to mine pops open, missing my face by a hair's breadth.

"My apologies, Miss Moon!" Rory Bombay

skillfully grasps my hand and prevents me from stumbling backward and almost certainly landing on my rear end in the muddy slush.

"Thank you. I'm pretty sure I would've been in a lot of trouble if I'd damaged this designer suit."

Rory glances at Silas and back to me. "Isn't it your suit? Do you have an overbearing valet?" He chuckles.

Silas steps forward and disengages my hand from Mr. Bombay's before he replies. "I'm sure you're familiar with Tanya. She's not a dry cleaner to be trifled with." He loops my arm through his elbow and gives me a meaningful tug. "Come on, Mitzy, we have business."

Rory calls down the alley, "Miss Moon, I was hoping I could take you to dinner in Grand Falls this evening."

I glance over my shoulder as Silas hustles me between the brick buildings and call, "I had to skip breakfast, so let's start with lunch and see what happens."

"Perfect. There's a lovely patisserie on 3rd Avenue. Why don't you change into something less restrictive and I'll meet you in front of the bookshop in half an hour?"

Just before Silas steers me around the corner, I shout, "It's a date."

"Mitzy, I thought your grandmother and I were quite clear about Mr. Bombay and his intentions."

I untangle my arm and stop on the sidewalk.

Silas takes two more steps before he realizes I'm not going to budge.

In my best grown-up voice, I announce, "I will take your recommendations under advisement. But I'm old enough to make my own decisions. And let's not forget I have more than the average sense of right and wrong."

Silas turns and walks toward me on the sidewalk. "Those extra senses are exactly what your grandmother and I are endeavoring to protect."

Now that sounded unduly ominous. But I refuse to give him the satisfaction of knowing that he got to me. "It's just lunch, Silas. We'll walk there, eat lunch, and walk back. I'm not getting in a car with him. I'm not spending the day with him. I'm not going away with him for the weekend. It's just lunch." Now that I think about it, the thought of going away with him for the weekend doesn't sound terrible.

"I hope you know what you're doing. However, I fear you do not." Silas walks me to the front door of the bookshop and bids me farewell.

I hurry inside, up the circular staircase, pull the candle handle next to *Saducismus Triumphatus,* and slip into my apartment as soon as the secret bookcase door slides open. I kick off my chunky heels and drop the suit on the floor as I rush into the closet to put on something more in line with my standard fare. Skinny jeans, UGGs, and, despite the cold, one of my favorite T-shirts. The slogan reads "Coffee is Magic" and it has a picture of a witch riding a stir stick over a mug of bubbling java. As I'm touching up my makeup, a sphere of light sparkles toward me and I gaze into the mirror, spellbound, as Grams materializes next to me. "Now that's more my speed." I sigh with relief.

"Well, you've been such a pill about my pop-ins, what choice do I have?" She chuckles and places her hand on my shoulder.

I still can't get used to the idea of actually being able to sense her touch. It's such a strange feeling. It's almost like a hand on my shoulder, but it's weightless and comforting at the same time.

"How did everything go at the school, dear?"

I finish applying my lip-gloss before I answer. "It went pretty well. I didn't trip and fall and I think my little speech was all right."

"What did you say?"

"Is it weird if I say I don't remember?" As I think back over the morning, I literally can't remember one word of my speech.

"That's perfectly normal. I gave a multitude of

public speeches in my day, and I can't remember a single one."

"Well, I'm not sixty-something and I'm still alive, so it seems like I should be able to remember what words come out of my mouth."

Grams seems to experience a flare in brightness. "Young lady, I didn't choose my ghost-age of thirty-five so that you could remind me how old I was when I died! Let's all just stick to the script, shall we?"

I turn and survey my circa-thirty-five-year-old grandmother and shake my head. "Yes, of course, Myrtle Isadora Johnson Linder Duncan Willamet Rogers. Let's make absolutely sure we're sticking to your script!"

I walk through her apparition and Grams swirls after me.

"Are you off to the diner for lunch?"

There's a hint of regret in her voice, and I can only imagine how much she misses Odell. They grew so close at the end of her life.

"Well, you know Odell—"

I point to my lips and shake my head.

"Sorry, dear. It's all so jumbled up. I'll do better, I promise."

"I'm actually having lunch at the patisserie on 3rd Avenue."

As hard as I try, I can't keep thoughts of the enticing, green-eyed Rory Bombay out of my mind. I push the plaster medallion and, just as the bookcase is about to slide open, Ghost-ma summons the strength to push the medallion a second time, slamming the bookcase closed. I spin around. "Grams! How rude."

"Silas and I warned you about him. What on earth are you thinking?"

"I'll tell you the same thing I told Silas. I'm a grown woman, and I can make my own decisions. It's just lunch." I push the medallion and this time, as soon as the door begins to slide open, I shove my foot in. It might seem reckless, but I don't think my angry Ghost-ma would actually risk injuring me.

The angry whoosh of an exhale followed by the swishing, swirling disappearance of Grams confirms my suspicion. I slip out of the apartment and down the stairs as my heart fills with blossoming anticipation. While I'm negotiating climbing over the "No Admittance" chain my lunch date is once again delayed.

"Hey, doll, you headed up to the diner?"

What is it with everyone assuming I can only eat at the diner? "I'm going to lunch, if that's what you're asking."

"Whooee, testy. Is Sheriff Erick still ignoring your many advances?" Twiggy stamps a biker-boot-clad foot and cackles with unnecessary abandon.

"Actually, my lunch date is a handsome, wealthy businessman."

"Well, la dee da, Your Highness. If that's the case, you might want to take the time to chew your food before you swallow." Yet another chuckle escapes from my volunteer employee.

"Wow, everyone is out to give me life lessons today. Did you need something, or did you just come out here for your own amusement?"

"You know how much I look forward to our little chats. But if it's not too much trouble, can you stop at Rex's and pick up some cello tape?"

I have no idea what cello tape is, but I'm not about to ask. "Sure. No problem." As I'm walking toward the front door, Twiggy issues a final warning.

"Don't let your guard down around that man. I know he seems charming, but any guy that handsome and slick-talkin' has got to have an ulterior motive."

I choose not to answer. I've had guys that handsome and even handsomer interested in me before. Hot single girls are few and far between in Sedona. Truth be told, hot single guys are fewer and farther between. Every single guy in Sedona is slathered in patchouli oil and carries a djembe drum! I honestly can't complain about the offerings in Pin Cherry Harbor. Sheriff Erick. Rory Bombay. Mitzy Moon has done all right for herself since she did a runner on her previous life and took up residence near this gorgeous great lake.

Rory is patiently waiting just outside the front door. He's leaned against the lamppost like a movie poster for a hit 1950s picture. His lovely fedora is raked at the perfect angle to emphasize his deep, brooding eyes. The collar of his thick wool overcoat is turned up against the chill and those sexy kidskin gloves hold—a present?

"Is that for me?"

Rory feigns surprise as he looks down at his own hand. "Oh my. What do we have here?" He turns over one hand and places the adorable gold package with its tiny silver bow in his palm. "I suppose you should open it and find out."

Not to harp on the foster-kid thing, but presents . . . They're a big deal! I snatch the present from his hand like a kid on Christmas morning. And by that, I mean the kids I've seen in movies that get presents on Christmas morning, because I wouldn't know from personal experience. "Thank you."

"You might want to wait until you've opened it, Miss Moon."

"What did I tell you?"

Rory smiles that crooked grin that makes my

insides gooey and chuckles. "I'm sure I meant to say Mitzy."

I undo the silver ribbon and open the perfect gold box. Inside is a delicate gold ring that wraps around a cat's-eye emerald. It's breathtaking, and definitely expensive. "Rory! I can't accept this."

"Of course you can. It just came in from a huge estate we're processing and I thought it would look lovely on your hand."

"But it looks really expensive. It just doesn't feel right."

"Nonsense. Consider it a token of our friendship. Now let's get some lunch." He takes the ring out of the box, pulls off my mitten, slips the ring on my right hand, and holds the mitten while I obediently slip my hand back inside. He slides the box and ribbon into his pocket and places my arm through the crook of his elbow.

As we walk across the street, I wonder if it would be rude to ask for the box. It was such a cute box and such a pretty shiny ribbon. Maybe it will come up at lunch. "So there's a bakery in Pin Cherry Harbor?"

"Patisserie, but yes. Where do you think Odell gets those pin cherry pies for the diner?"

"What? I thought he made them himself?"

"Odell? Making pie? Now that man is a genius

behind the grill, but I think that's where his skills end."

I'm a little offended by his low opinion of Odell. "That man" was the first friend I ever made when I came to Pin Cherry and he's been kind and generous to me every day since. I'd like to say as much, but I settle for, "I'm sure Odell could make a pie if he wanted to."

"No offense intended, Mitzy."

I'm starting to think Silas and Grams might've been partially right about Rory. Maybe he's a little too refined and a little too pompous for my taste. As we pass Myrtle's Diner, I purposely avert my gaze. I feel like I'm cheating on Odell by going to this fancy patisserie. Well, I'm pretty sure it's going to be a one-time thing and I'll never go back, and I'll probably never have lunch with Rory again either.

"Are you warm enough?"

"Yeah. My dad got me this coat and it's rated for like seventy below, I think."

"How is Jacob?"

I keep forgetting how small this town is and how much everyone knows about everyone else's business. But it shouldn't surprise me that a man like Rory would have knowledge of one of the largest robberies to happen in the northland in two decades. Sure, my dad's out of prison and he's an upstanding member of the community, now. But I bet there are plenty of people who still think the worst. "He's doing great. He inherited the Duncan estate and he's taken over at the train business—"

"Oh, I heard. Something about a convention in Chicago?" Rory snickers.

I forgot he was present at Odell's "surprise" news. I stop dead in my tracks and put my full weight into my heels.

Rory's elbow jerks against my arm and he comes to a stop, spinning around to stare at me in shock.

"Look, you don't know me that well, so I'm probably giving you more leeway than I should. But let me be perfectly clear, my family is the most important thing in my life and I'm not going to stand here and listen to some outsider make snide remarks and innuendos about my father. He's a decent guy and he paid his debt to society. So if this is going to continue"—I point back and forth between myself and Rory—"then you're going to need to change your tone of voice. Is that clear?" I don't remember exactly when I put my hands on my hips, but that's where they are.

"You're absolutely right, Mitzy. I only know what I've read in the papers or heard through local gossip. I don't know the whole story and I definitely have no business being flip with regard to your personal life. I certainly hope you'll forgive my crass comments and let me make it up to you over a steaming cup of hot chocolate and possibly the best chocolate croissant you'll ever eat."

Hot chocolate and croissants? How am I supposed to maintain my superior air of disinterest when faced with hot chocolate and baked goods? *Julie & Julia*, this guy is good. "I'm happy to give you the opportunity, Rory. Let's hope those croissants are as good as you say." I slip my arm back through his elbow and we make our way to the patisserie with only the sound of the crisp snow beneath our feet.

Despite the promise of hot chocolate and croissants, once we arrive at Bless Choux, Rory insists that I try a slice of their delectable quiche before we jump into dessert. I'm not a big fan of delayed gratification, but the coffee is divine and the flaky, buttery quiche crust could be one of the best things I've eaten in weeks. Odell forgive me. "This is delicious. Thanks for suggesting I switch up my routine."

"I'm so glad you're enjoying your lunch. I hope you will reconsider my offer to take you to dinner."

"Let's see how that hot chocolate pans out before we make any additional plans." I smile and take another sip of my coffee. As someone who's made hundreds, if not thousands, of cups of coffee at an insanely wide variety of coffee shops in the Southwest, I can tell you with a rather large degree of certainty that this is the best coffee I've ever tasted. There's a hint of vanilla and a subtle hazelnut finish. Truly satisfying.

"Perhaps if I give you some details it will help you make your decision. There's a lovely little restaurant in Grand Falls run by a former New York City chef. The hustle and bustle of the big city got to him and he chose to escape all the stress and open a little bistro. The restaurant is set in a converted Finnish pioneer homestead. There's a single seating, Thursday through Sunday nights, and the menu is different each night. The chef chooses his dishes based on local fare and seasonal availability of imported ingredients. The basement is a wine cellar filled with some of the finest bottles you will ever have the pleasure of gazing upon, let alone tasting. He serves hors d'oeuvres in the wine cellar, complete with pairings, about an hour before dinner. Then everyone is called up to the main floor and a five-course dinner is served, followed by a dessert course and digestifs or a pousse-café. I assure you it is an experience not to be missed. Yves Bistro. They have neither a website nor a phone. Reservations can only be made through personal acquaintance with the chef via his private cell phone number."

I am not at all used to the trappings of wealth. Everything that Rory just said sounds like a TV show that I might watch an episode of and then be so disgusted with all the hoity-toity flaunting of money that I would never watch it again. Of course, part of my disdain for money is that I never had any. Thinking back on how my inheritance helped me get out of a great deal of trouble at the high school, and how good it felt to donate money to the much-needed programs at the school, is starting to shift my perspective on wealth. Money can be used for good, and I suppose there's nothing wrong with enjoying a delicious meal with interesting company. I swallow my food before answering. See, I'm learning. "It sounds amazing. I am just not sure if I'm into that sort of thing."

"What sort of thing? Good food? Good company? A truly memorable evening?" Rory leans forward and strokes his finger along the back of my right hand. "I can promise you it will be a very memorable evening."

I hope he can't see the goosebumps on my arms or the way I'm sure my pupils have dilated. I was barely getting comfortable with the idea of having dinner with this man, and now he's making promises about memorable evenings. I'm going to have to get a hold of myself. I finish the last of my coffee and set down the cup. "I'll definitely consider it. It sounds lovely."

He turns my hand over gently and draws a

swirling line down my wrist as he practically purrs, "Are you ready for your hot chocolate?"

"Mmhmm." I feel flushed and words have abandoned me.

Rory walks toward the glass pastry case to place our order, and I promise you I try not to stare. But I can't help myself. His broad shoulders, that gorgeous sweater, and those tailored pants—probably a European cut—that fit in all the right places. Oh no, I'm gawking. I tear my eyes away and glance up and down the enticing display in the pastry case. I have to admit that, for the first time in a long time, I find the food less enticing than the company.

Rory returns with our chocolate croissants and moments later two steaming hot chocolates, with whip cream and chocolate shavings, are delivered to the table. There are only a few other patrons in the bakery, but I know from experience that our drinks must've been pushed to the top of the queue to be delivered so quickly

"Have you always had money?"

He tilts his head. "What an odd question."

"I don't know. You just seem really comfortable being rich. I never had money and this whole inheritance thing is a little unsettling. I mean, making that donation to the school this morning was the strangest feeling I've ever had. I kind of felt like a superhero."

"I think it's wonderful that you made a generous contribution to the high school. And to answer your question, I wasn't born into money. However, I knew from a very young age that I wanted to be financially comfortable and to have the kind of influence that wealth would provide."

It's an interesting and honest answer, but there's an edge in his voice that concerns me. "Did your parents resent the fact that you wanted to do better than them?"

"I'm not sure if 'resent' is the correct word. My father was a butcher and I think he just assumed I would follow in his footsteps."

"Is Bombay your real name?"

A strange crackle of energy storms in his eyes, and when his hand reaches across the table and touches mine, I feel a pull that is not of this world.

"It seems like we're venturing into second-date territory, Mitzy. I hope you'll consider that dinner invitation."

There's a heat on my skin where his fingers touch it. And suddenly there's more than that—a picture flashes into my mind of a building on fire. And then I hear the word "Beware." I lean back in my chair and pull my hand away. I try to be subtle but the muscle that tightens in Rory's angled jaw lets me know that I failed. "I'll definitely consider the invitation, thank you." I slide my chair back and slip into my coat. "I have to pick up a few things at the drugstore for Twiggy. Thank you so much for lunch. It was delicious, and I'm happy to know this place exists."

Rory stands and gives me a little bow with his head. "I also enjoyed our lunch, Mitzy. I hope you will allow me the pleasure of your company again, in the near future." And with that, he scoops up my right hand and kisses it.

I blush profusely under the jealous stares of the other patrons. Quickly slipping on my mittens, I hustle out the door without another word.

As I walk back to Main Street and Rex's, I fret about the psychic messages I received at the patisserie. Normally I would ask Silas or Grams to weigh in, but they've already made their opinions about Rory Bombay quite clear.

CHAPTER 15

THE CRUSHING GUILT of having stepped out on Odell by eating at Bless Choux forced me to eat a midnight microwave pizza last night. Even Pyewacket was uninterested in my leftovers. And the awesome side benefit of eating rubbery, irradiated, Italian food late at night is crazy weird dreams.

In spite of my strong position against rising early, by 5:30 a.m. I can no longer tolerate lying in bed and staring up at the moon-kissed ceiling.

I stumble into the bathroom with high hopes that an invigorating shower will hold me over until the diner opens at six.

The depressing, dull-grey light of the ungodly early morning only serves to reinforce my belief that nothing good comes from "getting the worm."

And I can assure you I'm not referring to the one at the bottom of a tequila bottle.

As I open the side door into the alley a blast of air hits me with such a frozen fury, I stumble backward and gasp for breath as the door slams shut. *"Polar Express!"* I'm not sure if that's what seventy below zero feels like, but I'm not going back for seconds without a whole lot more layers. I shiver my way upstairs and search through the lovely rows of built-in drawers in my mega closet.

"What are you looking for, honey?"

Since I've never been allowed in the closet unsupervised, part of me is expecting this pop-in. "Do you have any thermals? Is that the right word?"

"Of course, dear. You'll find the silk long underwear and sweaters in the fourth drawer down on the left.

Talk about your OCD. It seems like books weren't the only things Grams enjoyed collecting.

"Ahem."

I chuckle as I open the drawer and locate the long underwear. I peel off all my layers and re-dress with the proper base coat of insulation. I put on something called a "turtleneck" under my T-shirt and nearly suffocate before I figure out how to fold down the ridiculously long neck. "From what I know about turtles, Grams, their necks are way more functional than this. I feel like this should be called a spiderweb neck to accurately describe the way it clings to you and threatens to trap you inside its strangling web."

Grams laughs so hard she ghost-snorts, which sends me into a fit of my own early-morning lack-of-sleep giggles.

"Oh dear, I'm super punchy. I better get down to the diner and get some coffee in my system before I crash."

Grams is still recovering, but manages to blurt, "You're such a hoot! What else is on your agenda today?"

"Absolutely nothing. I mean, I think I'll organize the murder wall—which is technically a "hit-and-run wall" this time—and see if I can come up with any more ideas about Doc Ledo's case. But after that, Pyewacket and I will have a long nap."

"All right, dear. You say hello to Odell for me won't you?"

I hesitate and I can feel my Ghost-ma's profound sadness when she realizes her mistake. I turn and smile wistfully.

"He knows how much you cared about him, Grams. I think it would almost break his heart all over to know that your spirit is still here but has no way to communicate with him. He has a lot of fond memories of your last year on this side of the veil. I think it's probably best we leave those untouched."

Little glistening, ethereal tears spring from the corners of her eyes. "You really do have to figure out a way to get me a handkerchief, dear. Gosh, I miss him. There are so many times in my life that I wondered what it would've been like if I'd gotten sober sooner and stayed with him. Can you imagine? Me with only one husband?"

"Everything you did brought you to me, Grams. Remember? No regrets. No do overs. One day at a time. Right?"

She takes a shaky breath and nods. "Of course. We're all just doing the best we can with what we have. The wisdom to know the difference, that's what I learned."

My stomach growls with unnatural ferocity. "Oh, I better get down to the diner."

Grams chuckles and floats over to the zonked-out Pyewacket.

I sigh. "Sure, now he can sleep. All night long he was prowling along the windowsills and growling at the wind. As soon as I get up, he sleeps like a baby."

"You know, Mitzy, babies don't actually sleep that well. Your father was a colicky baby and he kept me up for most of the first year of his life. I'll never forget the first time he slept through the night. I think that's when I started to believe in magic!"

"Seems like you're a bit of a hoot yourself, Grams. Must run in the family." I leave the apartment feeling tired, hungry, and full of the warmth of belonging. But regardless of how prepared I thought I was, when I open the door into the alleyway and catch that icy wind knifing across the lake it still takes my breath away. I fight against the invisible force of what must be a one-hundred-mile-an-hour gust, and manage to get the door closed. The cold propels me to the diner in record time.

As I push open the door and make my blustery entrance, I'm suddenly reminded of my first day in Pin Cherry Harbor. All eyes turn to the door, including Tally and Odell. But instead of silent, unwelcome stares, today's result is far better.

"Good morning, Mitzy," Tally calls as she pours steaming coffee into a fresh mug, which I hope is for me.

Odell salutes me with his metal spatula through the red-Formica-trimmed orders-up window, and I take a seat at the empty counter.

"Special?"

"Done."

Tally sets down my coffee and waits expectantly.

"I'm sorry I don't have more information for you, Tally. But I've at least uncovered the fact that there was an eyewitness to the accident. I shared the information with Erick—Sheriff Harper—and hopefully he'll turn up a lead before me."

Tally blinks back tears and nods hopefully. "I know you're doing your best. I sure do appreciate you looking into things."

"Of course. Anything for Doc Ledo. Me and Pyewacket owe him." I smile and nod encouragingly.

Tally nods briefly before hurrying into the back.

Odell shakes his head. "It's been tough on her. But I know you'll figure this out. You're smarter than the average bear."

I have no information about the intelligence of bears so I'm not sure if that's a compliment, but I give him the old "nod and smile."

"I didn't see you for lunch or supper yesterday? Are you on one of those new fad diets or somethin'?"

I knew this question was coming and I hope my answer passes muster. "After the whole presentation at the school yesterday, I received a lunch invitation, then I ended up crashing for most of the afternoon and had to eat a terrible microwaved disc of probably-not-pepperoni for dinner. Don't worry, I paid the price. Now I'm back at the best restaurant in town, and not likely to make those mistakes again."

Odell chuckles as his spatula scrapes across the grill with the confidence of a seasoned professional.

"I do have one question, if you don't mind?"

"Questions are free; answers could cost you."

"Fair enough. My lunch companion said that you don't make your own pin cherry pie. He said it comes from the bakery on 3rd Avenue. That true?"

Odell locks eyes with me through the orders-up window, slowly sets down his spatula, and walks out of the kitchen with an unhurried but singular purpose. He places both hands on the counter, takes a deep breath, and replies, "My pin cherry pie is made from my great-grandma's recipe. It's won the grand prize at the Pin Cherry Festival every year except 1983, when my mother was too sick to bake and I unsuccessfully tried my hand."

"Understood. Clearly my lunch companion was misinformed."

"Your lunch companion, as you call him, is misinformed about a lot of things. I can't be the first one to tell you to watch yourself around that man."

So much for secrecy. Clearly Odell knows whom I had lunch with and most likely where we had that lunch. "Correct. You are not the first. Silas, Gr— Twiggy, everyone. Everyone seems to think Rory Bombay is bad news. Maybe you're all right and I'm wrong. But all I know is he's been a perfect gentleman and I have no reason to suspect him of anything besides wanting to get to know me." Now, I realize that's not entirely true if we take my psychic warnings into consideration. But that's just between my mood ring and me right now, and I don't intend on sharing those messages with anyone until I get a little more information.

"You're a grown woman, Mitzy. Just keep your head on a swivel, all right?"

"Copy that. You better check on my breakfast. I like my eggs scrambled hard—not burned."

Odell snickers and wanders back to the grill, mumbling under his breath about young ladies trying to tell him how to run his restaurant, or something like that.

Back at the apartment, I have my tacks and my green yarn at the ready, and I'm staring absently at the two items pinned on my hit-and-run investigation wall, which is, of course, not the actual wall because Twiggy doesn't want me making holes with tacks in the lath and plaster. So really it's more of a hit-and-run corkboard, but that doesn't sound very investigate-y. Oh, and I have to use green yarn instead of red, because Grams said red reminds her of blood and makes her uncomfortable.

Anyway, I'm sitting in my scalloped-back chair staring at the article about Ledo's accident pinned on the left and the article about the stolen angel statue tacked on the right. I take out my three-by-five index cards and write "Angel Thief is the witness," and I tack that card dead center. With string leading from one article to the angel thief card to the other article I've established my connection. Now all I need is to figure out who is the angel thief.

I pace down the span of six-by-six windows and marvel at the crazy bright blue sky appearing behind the clouds. Apparently this insane wind is clearing out the cloud cover and revealing a truly magnificent winter scene. I stop and stare out over the frozen, snow-covered lake and blink as the sun sparkles like diamonds off thick white powder and dazzles my vision.

Back to the case. The footprint in the snow was definitely a DC skateboard shoe. The size and brand absolutely—most likely—guarantee the thief was a high-school student. The occupant of the house and owner of the statue is Brynley's grandmother. Brynley is the kind of terrible high-school mean girl who strikes fear into the hearts of her fellow students. The list of people who would like to knock her down a peg promises to be rather long.

I need to find motive. A deeper driving force.

My mood ring seems to turn to ice on my left hand. I risk a glance. The ring is blue-grey and my hand feels heavy. My heart feels heavy. I feel so sad.

I stare into the polished cabochon as the blue-grey swirls away to reveal an angel statue.

Shivers shoot through my body and I have trouble swallowing. I've never seen the statue. This has to be important. This information is—

"Mitzy? Mitzy, are you okay?"

I turn away from the windows and I can't see Grams. My mind's eye is filled with the image of the memorial statuary.

"Grams? I can't make the vision stop. What do I do? I can't see anything else."

"Sit down on the floor, sweetie. Try to sit down. Close your eyes. Take a deep breath and try to focus on this room. You're safe. You're in your apartment. Take another deep breath."

I slide down against the wall and desperately try to focus on the sound of my grandmother's voice. My heart hurts so much. I want that statue. I need that statue. I gasp for air and my eyelids fly open. "Grams! I saw the statue and I thought I was experiencing the widow's feelings, but it was the— I think I felt the— thief!"

CHAPTER 16

I BLINK SLOWLY. My vision is blurry and there is a halo of light hugging the edges of everything. I feel like every patient waking from a coma in every movie I've ever watched.

I wiggle my fingers and toes. Somehow I'm in my bed. Did I faint?

"No, sweetie. You had an episode."

My mouth doesn't want to work, so I'll have to settle for Grams' thought reading.

How did I get in bed?

"I coaxed you to walk over and take off the ring."

I rub the fingers of my left hand together and my ring finger feels naked. *Why?*

"I think you just got too much information at once. Do you remember anything?"

I struggle to blink away the hazy sparkles and think back—

"Keep breathing, Mitzy."

I take a deep breath and force myself to sit up. I slap my cheeks and try to clear my head. "I felt the emotions of the thief, but they're not here. I don't think I've ever gotten a remote feeling. Is that what you'd call it?"

"I have no idea. You'd better call Silas."

I rub my eyes and slide my legs out from under the covers. But they don't quite come out; instead they get tangled in my expensive Egyptian cotton sheets and I fall out of bed onto my head. "Ouch!"

Grams swirls nervously over me.

"Well, my head's clear now." I stand and reach for the ring.

Ghost-ma rushes between my outstretched hand and the mood ring resting on my nightstand. "I wouldn't. Not until you talk to Silas."

"Fair enough." I search the room for my cell.

"I think you left it on the vanity, in the bathroom."

I point to my lips and shake my head. "I'm fully operational now, Grams. Thought-dropping is once again off limits."

"Of course, dear."

Why does it always sound like she's patronizing me rather than complying?

"It's just—" Grams slaps a ring-ensconced hand over her mouth.

"Yeah, now I remember why."

I grab my phone and call my solicitor. Listen to all those grown up words. Phone (that actually has service) and solicitor (like I'm fancy).

"Good afternoon, Mitzy."

I take a moment to remember my manners. "Good afternoon, Silas. I had an episode and Grams said you should come over."

"A feeling?"

"It was like being trapped in a movie in someone else's mind. I—"

"I shall be there posthaste."

SILENCE.

"He hung up on me!" I look at Grams and shake my head. "Mr. Manners hung up on me."

"Oh dear, it must be serious. You should drink some water and have a seat."

I'm too woozy to argue. I walk into the bathroom and slurp some water from the faucet.

A "tsk-tsk" echoes from the main room.

Wiping my mouth with the back of my hand, I venture a peek at my reflection.

The sallow skin and vacant eyes that stare back at me do not look familiar. A memory slams into my consciousness. "Grams, didn't you say that trying to wield too much power is what made you sick?"

"As I explained, honey, the doctors always said it was liver failure, but I knew better."

"How's that?"

"I was never satisfied with clairvoyance alone. I wanted the other gifts too. I wanted what you have and I pushed myself too hard."

"Look at me." I point to my deathly pale complexion. "Is it happening to me?"

"You lie down and we'll see what Silas has to say."

I shake my head and collapse onto the thick down comforter. Seems like Grams is being rather evasive. I'd say it must be as bad as it looks.

The bookcase door slides open and Silas—uncharacteristically—rushes in. "Twiggy was busy tending to a customer, so I made my own way."

From my perch on the four-poster bed, I wave weakly. "Hey, Silas."

He slips his magicked spectacles from an inner pocket and hooks the ends of the wire arms around his ears. "Ah, Isadora. Is it serious?"

Grams nods furiously.

Huh. Seems a little different than the dodgy answer she gave me.

Silas leans over me. Blinks his huge eyes behind the bespelled-glasses, before removing them and placing them in his coat pocket. "Now, let's see what we have." He scans my face and he picks up my left hand. I feel alternating chills and heat on my skin. His eyes dart to the ring on the nightstand. "You were wearing your grandmother's ring when this happened?"

"Yup."

He reaches for my right hand. "And this? Is this yours, Isadora?"

I swallow hard and feel an unbridled compulsion to lie.

Grams shakes her head and then notices that Silas is not wearing his spectacles. "Mitzy, he can't see me. Tell him it's not my ring."

Silas strokes his mustache and looks at me. "What does she say?"

"She doesn't remember," I lie.

"Mizithra Achelois Moon! What on earth are you doing? Where did you get that ring?"

I force myself to think about french fries and how much I love them. But that leads me to thinking about Odell, which leads to a snippet of regret about the patisserie, which sends me right to—

"Mitzy! You tell Silas about that devil Rory Bombay this instant, or I swear I will—"

"All right! All right." I wave Silas away and slide my legs off the side of the bed. I want to walk away from this alchemist before I spill the beans.

"You look unstable. Are you having another episode?"

The concern in his voice breaks my heart.

"As it well should," snaps Grams.

I plop onto the overstuffed ottoman and mumble, "Rory gave it to me."

Silas whips out his glasses, fixes them over his ears, and searches the room. "Isadora, did she say the ring was a gift from Mr. Bombay?"

I scowl at Grams' traitorous nod.

Silas approaches and the stooped, scuffling old man transforms into a commanding force. "Give me the ring."

"Easy, Gollum." I twist desperately at the ring, but my finger is swollen and I can't get it off. "It's stuck."

"I told you that man was dangerous!" Grams anxiously circles.

"It's not like magically stuck, Grams. My finger is swollen from lying around all day and I can't get it off.

"Allow me." Silas takes my hand, without permission, and mumbles something as he marks a symbol on my wrist with his finger.

The gesture fills me with a dreadful déjà vu.

He easily slides the ring from my finger and slips it in his pocket. "There. I'll examine it more thoroughly in my study. I have some specialized tools."

I stare at my slightly thinner finger and whistle, "Boy, if you could bottle that spell you'd have women lining up around the block." I absently rub my bodacious hips.

"It is not a spell, Mitzy. Alchemy is the transmutation of matter."

"Whatever you say." I stare at the bare finger and wonder if there's anything to my episode and Rory's gift.

Grams nods once and crosses her arms over her chest.

Before she can launch into a lecture, the dulcet tones of Twiggy crackle over the intercom. "You got some punk kid down here says you're his friend and asked him to stop by the bookshop."

"*Sweet Home Alabama!*" I jump up and run to the bathroom. Splashing water on my face does absolutely nothing. I still look like warmed-over death.

"What is it? Who's here?" Grams seems more frantic than me.

"It's this kid, Stellen, from the high school. He already thinks I'm a little nuts. I can't let him see me like this."

"But why is he here, honey?"

"Because of me and the undercover thing. I said 'friends' and now I have to . . . Someone stall him!"

Count on Silas to keep cool under pressure. "I'll engage the young man in discourse while you two put Mitzy in order."

"Great. GO!" I push Silas toward the door and dive back into the bathroom.

"Don't panic, dear. We can make a silk purse out of this sow's ear in no time. You get busy with that makeup and I'll see what I can find in the closet."

I shout through the wall after my vanishing grandmother, "Nothing too fancy. Keep it casual. He's a kid."

I dump the makeup bag out on the marble countertop and grab wildly. Concealer, foundation, lip tint, blush . . . Dear lord, I look like a Goth.

Muffled chuckles from the closet do nothing to improve my self-esteem.

Two coats of mascara and a ton of blush later, my face looks almost human. But this hair . . . What am I going to do about this hair?

"How about a nice stocking cap?"

I shake my head at my reflection and walk into the closet. "What the heck is a stocking cap?"

"It's a very fashionable knit hat. There's a variety in the top drawer over there, below the jackets."

I slide open the drawer and grin. Imagine this: cover-up my haystack of white hair with an awesome hat! This is genius. How have I not been wearing hats my whole life? I pull out a red slouchy number and slip it on. Turning toward Grams, I ask, "How do I look?"

Grams chuckles. "Adorable as always. Isn't there some kind of song about a strawberry hat?"

"If you mean 'Raspberry Beret,' then yes. But as far as I know there are no other fruit/hat related songs." It's good to laugh and I feel a little energy surging back into my limbs. "All right. Hat? Check. Makeup? Check. What am I wearing?"

Grams gestures to my black skinny jeans and a striped cashmere boyfriend sweater, which I've come to love. "How about this? Casual, but classy."

"Does it go with the hat?"

"I think there's a matching scarf that will pull it all together."

"Maybe it's just because I'm from Arizona, but do people wear scarves indoors?"

"Oh, it's all the rage once you get up north."

I rummage through the drawer and find the matching scarf. I'm dressed in a flash and scampering down the metal stairs.

"I think I hear her thundering our way now," announces Twiggy.

"Hey, Stellen, sorry I wasn't prepared. I hope Silas kept you entertained."

Stellen nods and takes a couple of steps back. "Hey, Miss Moon."

"Well, now that you've arrived, I shall take my leave. A pleasure to meet you, Mr. Jablonski."

"Okay." Stellen grins nervously.

Silas harrumphs, for what I'm assuming is the loss of civility in today's youth, and shuffles out the front door.

"So, what would you like to see first?"

"Do you really have a caracal?"

"I really do. Although I haven't seen him since this morning. Which is odd, because he usually enjoys barging into my every private moment. Let's have a look around the bookshop and see if we can find him." I start down the first aisle, looking high and low, ready for a sneak attack from either direction. However, no books are pushed on my head and no fiendish fur ball leaps out from between the books. By the time we make it to the back room, I'm actually growing concerned. "Twiggy, have you seen Pye?"

"Yep."

I look at Stellen and shrug. He smiles conspiratorially. "And can you tell me where you saw him?"

"Yep."

Stellen snickers.

"Where did you see him?"

Twiggy slowly rotates her office chair away

from the computer screen and toward my voice. "Now you're asking the right questions. I saw him up in the Rare Books Loft down at the far end of the balcony. He followed me up there when I was shelving books this morning, and I never saw him come down."

"Thank you." I say it sarcastically, but I'm pretty sure you already figured that out. "Come on, Stellen, let's go find us a cat."

We walk over to the circular staircase and I unhook the "No Admittance" chain.

A disembodied voice shouts from the back room, "You hook that right back up behind yourselves."

"Copy that."

I roll my eyes for Stellen's benefit and he chuckles. We hustle up the steps and down to the far end of the balcony. There on the floor beneath the tall ladder crouches the ever-vigilant Pyewacket. He takes one look at Stellen and hisses dramatically.

"Don't worry, it's not you. He's not good with new people."

"Wow. It's true. I've never seen one in real life."

I walk toward Pyewacket and crouch down. "What's up, buddy? Don't you want to meet my new friend?"

"Ree-ow." Soft but condescending.

"What did he say?"

"It's not an exact science. Near as I can tell, he's ambivalent. Maybe sit down on the floor and see if he finds that less threatening."

Stellen quickly sits down and folds his hands quietly.

That's when I see the bottom of his shoes.

"RE-OW!" Game on! Pyewacket launches from his hiding place and thwacks Stellen's shoe furiously, before he rockets across the mezzanine.

Stellen gasps with amazement. "Wow, he's fast. How cool. That cat is lit."

"Hey, are those DCs?" I gesture to his shoes. I really wish I had my mood ring on right now, but even without it I notice the change in Stellen's posture.

"Yeah, everyone has them."

"Yeah, I figured." Something tells me there's more to this story and I think I'm going to hate myself for pushing, but here goes. "Do you want to see something really cool?"

Stellen gets to his feet and shifts his weight uncomfortably. "I guess, but I should probably get going."

"All right. It'll just take a minute."

We walk down the narrow curve of the balcony toward the wider mezzanine and the candle handle to my secret apartment. I reach up and tilt the candle down and the bookcase door slides open.

Stellen gasps. "It's like an episode of Scooby Doo!"

I laugh. "Right?"

He steps forward and peers into the apartment. He looks to the right and surveys the furniture and the built-in bookcases, and then he looks to the left and sees my hit-and-run wall. I'm just about to explain myself when he steps back and looks at me with the strangest combination of guilt and fear in his eyes. "I gotta go." He races down the circular staircase, easily hopping over the chain and running right out the front door.

I think I just got a break in my case. And it's literally the worst thing that's happened to me all week.

CHAPTER 17

AFTER A LONG DEPRESSING chat with Grams, we unanimously agree that I have to pursue the lead, but that I'll do everything I can to minimize the impact on Stellen's young life. The kid just doesn't strike me as a criminal. He must've had a good reason for taking the statue. And even though he's not a member of the "Brynley Fan Club," I refuse to believe that he was motivated solely by spite.

Time to put the wheels in motion with a call to my lawyer. "Silas, I have a situation." I put the call on speaker, so Grams can hear what he has to say.

"Good afternoon to you, too, Mitzy. I sincerely hope it doesn't have anything to do with Mr. Bombay."

Grams rushes in and blurts her concern.

I update him. "Grams wants me to tell you that

it has nothing to do with Rory. I got a lead on the angel statue and I need a home address for the taxidermist. That Jablonski kid's dad."

Silas asks for a moment to make some phone calls and says he'll get back to me as soon as possible.

Grams spirals and I pace as we wait for my phone to ring. When the "ring" finally comes, I nearly jump out of my skin and Grams scatters like smoke in the wind.

"Silas, did you get an address? Okay . . . Okay . . . I have to go alone . . . Well, it's not like she can— All right. I said all right. Yes, I'll call you when I get back." I press end and shake my head. "You'd almost think he doesn't trust me."

"Did he get you the address, dear?"

"Yes, but Silas says he's not pleased with the idea of me going out to the Jablonski property without an escort. He said he agrees only with 'extreme prejudice.'"

"You'd better get going. I'd hate for that child to do anything else he'll regret."

With the sun setting by 4:30 p.m. at this latitude, I bundle up with extra layers for my after-dark mission.

"Silas told me to leave my phone. And for you to call him if I'm not back by 9:00 p.m."

Grams floats slowly down from the ceiling like a

feather on a light breeze. "Call him? How should I call him, honey?"

I place my cell phone on the nightstand and begin Ghost-ma cell-phone lessons. "You see this little indentation here?"

She nods.

"You press that. See how the screen lights up?"

"Yes, I see it."

"All right. I'll open up the contacts and find Silas's number so that you can just press this green button and it will call him. You got that?"

"Of course. I've used a cell phone before, dear."

"I know, but not as a ghost. Do you think you can do it?"

"I opened the bookcase door the other day, remember?"

"Right. But I think you actually closed it, if I remember correctly. Which was a slightly creepy vengeful spirit thing to do."

Grams whirls away in a snit. "Well, you left me no choice."

"I believe it was my wise grandmother who once said, 'You always have a choice.'"

Grams does not respond. I can't honestly blame her. That was a low blow.

The faint sound of ghostly agreement drifting down from above.

"All right. I'm leaving the phone here. I'm

taking the mood ring, and if I'm not back by nine o'clock . . . You know what to do."

"Go easy on him, Mitzy. He's just a boy."

I nod, wrap one more loop of scarf around my neck, and zip up my thick coat.

The moonlit drive out to the Jablonski property only serves to double down on the ominous and eerie nature of my mission. Without the GPS app on my cell phone, I worry that I could become utterly lost. The art of map reading has definitely skipped my generation. But I'm getting a crash course tonight and I'm extremely grateful for the brilliant moonlight.

I make the final turn by the crumbling silo—excellent landmark—and thick trees arch over the road, blocking out the moon. Now I'm faced with being able to see only what my headlights illuminate, and, as the road narrows to a single track through the deep snow, I'm beginning to feel like I might have driven into the middle of a scary movie.

When I break out of the tree cover and my headlights shine on the Jablonski home, it does nothing to calm my nerves.

The dark and dreary cabin looks like every building you've ever seen in a teen horror film. I can almost hear the plodding footsteps of the approaching menace. I shut off the engine and step out of the car. Before I've even taken two steps, a deep voice echoes through the still night and turns my blood to ice.

"What's your business?"

I try to swallow, but my throat is so tight. I pivot slightly and see the shadow of a large man holding something very dead in one hand and something very dangerous in the other. I really hope that's not a gun. I know it is. But by hoping it's not, somehow I can keep myself from fainting. "Mr. Jablonski?"

"You from the school?"

At this point in the storm, I'll climb on any life raft offered. "Yes, yes. From the school." My vocal cords are so constricted by fear that I can barely get the words out. "Stellen?"

"In the house." He gestures with the barrel of his gun. "I just caught this striped skunk. Gonna skin 'em and prep the hide for tomorrow. You wanna watch?"

The blood-curdling scream clawing its way up my throat does not want to be suppressed. But if I have any hope of saving this doomed mission, I have to get over myself. I take a deep breath and remind myself that this is not a movie and this man is just a taxidermist. A taxidermist holding an enormous gun and a dead animal. Deep breath. Deep breath. "Oh, thank you for the generous offer." I can barely force the words past the gagging sensation. "But I think I'll head into the house and chat with Stellen. You, however . . . good luck with that."

"Alrighty then. He's not causing any trouble at school, is he?"

"Absolutely not. He's a very bright boy."

With a low, guttural grumble, Mr. Jablonski stomps off toward an outbuilding and it's all I can do to keep from sprinting to the cabin.

I knock firmly on the door.

The door creaks open and the dim light from a single bulb outlines the boy.

He tries to push the door shut, but I shove my foot in the narrowing opening. "Stellen. I'm not here to get you in any kind of trouble. Is there somewhere we can talk? Please. I promise you I'm not here about the theft."

The door groans open and the light hits the side of Stellen's face. Even in the semi-darkness, I can see his eyes are red and swollen.

"I honestly don't care about the statue. Can we talk?"

"Hold on."

He disappears into the murky interior and returns bundled for the outdoors. So much for my dream of having the conversation inside the slightly-warmer-than-outside cabin.

Stellen pushes past me and marches off into the blue-white moon-glazed snow. The rhythmic crunch-kick, crunch-kick, crunch-kick of his boots in the snow is the only sound penetrating the silence.

Since we're walking away from his father's animal-skinning outbuilding, I follow with slightly less trepidation. Like I said, I don't think this kid is a criminal and if he is I certainly hope I can overpower a sixteen-year-old boy, if it comes to that.

He ducks into a thick stand of small pine trees, almost like a Christmas tree farm, and I swallow loudly before I follow.

On the other side of the trees is a clearing bathed in a pool of almost-silver gloaming from the lunar reflection. There's a small log bench, clearly hewn by hand, and in the middle of the clearing— an angel.

The sight physically stops me in my tracks. The statue is so heartbreakingly beautiful that I honestly expect it to stretch out its wings and bless us both before ascending.

Stellen sits down on the bench and hangs his head in his hands.

I solemnly approach and ask, "Can I sit down?"

He makes a noncommittal sound, so I sit.

"What is this place?"

His voice is thick with emotion. "I call it my memory meadow."

The heavy sadness and the aching need for the

statue wash over me with such intensity that I can't stop myself from crying. "Can you tell me?"

"She was really sick. For a long time."

"Your mom?"

He nods silently.

I know Pin Cherry Harbor is way past where Jesus lost his sandals, but even I don't think they would allow the family to bury Mrs. Jablonski on their property.

As though he knows what I'm thinking, Stellen mumbles, "She's not buried here. Chuckwalla is buried here, but the statue is for both of them."

"Was Chuckwalla a pet?" I hope I got that right. It doesn't sound like a very human name, but these days who can be sure?

Stellen leans back and, for the first time tonight, I see him smile through his tears. "My mom gave him to me as a puppy. He had such a wide body and a cute little round belly . . . He was really the best dog ever. And every time I looked at him, I felt like she was still here, you know?"

"I absolutely do." I can't help thinking about losing my own mother. It would have given me so much comfort to have something she gave me, something alive, to remind me of her.

"It's just— Brynley's always bragging about how much money she has and how much her grandma spoils her because she was her grampa's favorite.

She kept showing pictures of the statue to everyone at school. I wasn't trying to hurt anyone. I just wanted—"

"I get it. I totally get it. Does your dad know?"

Stellen's face turns to a rictus of horror. "You're not going to tell him?"

"Never." I hurriedly change the subject. "Did you bury the dog by yourself?"

"He wanted to take Chuckwalla into that stupid shed and cut him— I couldn't let him. I needed to lay him to rest. Honor him, you know?"

"Yeah, I know." I look around the meadow and I can feel that there is something deeply magical here. But more than one life has been affected by recent events, and somehow I have to try to strike a balance. "Stellen, did you see the accident?"

A fresh set of muffled sobs shakes his hunched shoulders. "Yeah."

Relief floods through my body. "Can you describe the vehicle?"

"Yeah. It was an old 1980 Chevy pickup truck, blue and white, lifted."

The specificity surprises me. "How can you be so sure of the year and everything?"

He doesn't look up. "1980 was the only year of the square-body Chevy trucks that had the egg-crate grill."

Some kids are into video games. I guess this one

is into Chevy trucks. "And you saw it hit the doctor?"

Stellen shakes his head and proceeds to tell me the strangest tale I've ever heard. In the end, the only thing I know for sure is that I have to tell Erick what I've uncovered. And I absolutely have to keep Stellen out of it. "You know I have to tell Sheriff Harper what you saw."

"Do you think I'll go to jail?"

"I don't plan on giving him your name. I'll tell him I have to protect my sources, or something."

Stellen chuckles bitterly. "Too bad you don't work for the paper."

The mood ring on my left hand almost shocks me with the intensity of the electric jolt that shoots up my arm. I'd like to think I cover it up rather well by giving an exaggerated shiver. "You really are a genius. I tell you what, can you return that statue without getting caught?"

He looks at me like I'm crazy. "No way. The only reason it worked the first time was because everyone was at the Yuletide thing."

"Right." I had forgotten about everyone being at the Extravaganza. "New plan. You help me load that thing in my Jeep, tonight, and I'll keep you out of the story completely. Deal?"

He looks out over the meadow and fresh tears fill his eyes. "It's just—"

"You and I will head over to Broken Rock this weekend and we'll get a proper statue for Chuckwalla. Not trying to reward you for your crime, but I'd like to reward you for doing the right thing for Doc Ledo. Make sense?"

He nods. "Can I have a minute? To . . . you know?"

"Of course. I'll wait on the trail on the other side of the trees." I take one last look at this dreamscape and slide through the pine trees—back into the real world.

CHAPTER 18

BACK AT THE bookshop after a slow, silent drive through this otherworldly, glowing snow-covered landscape. I quietly let myself in the side door from the alley and, with a heavy heart, make my way upstairs to the mezzanine. As soon as I pull the candle handle, Grams practically explodes through the wall.

"Oh, thank goodness! I really wasn't sure I was going to be able to work that phone. I was so worried that my sporadic and unreliable ghostly abilities would abandon me when I needed them most." She circles around me, stops, and puts a hand over her mouth. "Dear! You've been crying."

I nod as I walk into the apartment, peeling off my winter layers as I go. "Give me a sec, Grams." I crawl directly into bed, with my clothes on, before I make the call. "Hey, Silas, I'm back at the apartment. I've got you on speakerphone, so let me get you and Grams up to speed, together."

I carefully lay out the details of my visit to what I describe as the filming location for a horror movie, and after setting the stage with the proper level of fear; I proceed to break their hearts in equal measure with the story of Stellen's memory meadow.

Grams clutches one of her many strands of pearls and sighs. "Poor little lamb."

Silas takes another approach. "Speaking as your lawyer, Mitzy, you must dispense of the stolen property before you share your lead with Sheriff Harper."

"He's right, you know? Erick isn't going to stand for you holding out. He'll force you to name the eyewitness." Grams shakes her head in concern.

"Actually, Stellen gave me the perfect idea. First thing tomorrow morning, I'm going to head over to the *Pin Cherry Harbor Post* and sign on as a freelance reporter. Nothing like the fourth estate to insulate my right to protect my sources."

Grams claps her ghostly hands and I can hear Silas chuckling on his end of the phone.

"You are a dastardly force to be reckoned with, Mitzy. I concur that the Shield Law will protect your journalistic sources, but just to be sure I've made myself clear, please drop off the statue to

Mrs. Jorgenson on your way to the newspaper office."

"All right. Fine. The thing is, I don't actually have a cover story for the statue reappearing."

"I recommend you focus on how fortunate it was that you happened upon it and leave before her profuse gratitude is replaced by any questions."

"Will do." I yawn loudly. "You two better let me get some sleep. It sounds like I'm going to have a very busy day tomorrow."

The crisp morning light seeps through my eyelids as Pyewacket head butts me.

"Good morning to you too, my furry fiend." I scratch him between his tufted ears and he purrs loudly. Clearly he's pleased to have once again directed my investigation. "Yes, Pyewacket, you are the smartest kitty. Now, do you happen to know who owns a 1980 blue-and-white Chevy pickup truck?"

He nips gently at my hand and I pull away in mock pain. "Ouch! You little demon! Fine. Thank you for your help. There'll be no further expectations." I walk toward the door and call back, "Come on, let's get your breakfast. I've got a very long to-do list."

As I chug my industrial-strength coffee and

power through a bowl of Fruity Puffs, Pyewacket's vengeful stare tracks every movement of my spoon. I may be taking my life into my hands here, but I can't risk going to the diner and spilling the beans before I have all my ducks in a row. Beans. Ducks. Uffda! (A local term of exasperation, which I've come to love.) It's too early for all this clandestine activity.

Back upstairs I work on making myself presentable, perhaps even a little adorable, since I will have the pleasure of seeing Erick today. Dressed for success, and brutal winter weather, I drive toward Olga Jorgensen's.

As I pull into the driveway at 1874 Pin Cherry Lane I rehearse my speech, especially my exit strategy.

I put the Jeep in "park" and open the rear hatch. The angel statue is a lot heavier than I remember, and the last thing I want to do is drop the ball on the five-yard line. I'm not a sports nut or anything, but I think the analogy holds up. "Put your back into it, Moon." My inner coach gives a little pep talk while I lift with my legs and heave the statue out of the back. I peer around the wings as I awkwardly stumble toward the front door. Setting the angel down on the corner of the porch, I turn it toward the door so the lovely inscription is visible, before ringing the doorbell.

The door swings open and the frail woman smiles up at me. As I'm about to launch into my well-rehearsed speech, she pushes open the storm door and exclaims, "It's back! It's back!" She rushes past me and embraces the angel statue.

I don't think I'm going to get a better out than this. "Is Brynley here?"

The woman turns around with tears in her eyes, "Oh no, dear, Brynley's at school. Shouldn't you be at school, Sadie?"

Uh oh, time to backpedal and make my exit. "Of course. I got stuck in my driveway and I was running totally late. But I'll catch up with her at school. Thanks." I turn and hustle it back to my car.

As I back out of the driveway, I see Olga inspecting every inch of the statue and pressing her hand to her heart. You know what? I'm glad she thinks it's a miracle. To me, that's even better.

There's no one at the front desk of the newspaper. Not that I'm surprised. I ring the little bell several times before Mr. Knudsen wanders out of the back and looks at me with slack-jawed surprise.

"Is anyone helping you?"

I can't stop from looking over my shoulder to see if there was someone I missed, but seeing no one beside myself, I launch into my objective. "Hi, Mr. Knudsen, I was really hoping to do some reporting for the newspaper. Do you use freelancers?"

His eyes blink behind his glasses in what I have come to understand as the mechanism that fuels his thought process.

"We don't really have assignments. You know my grandfather . . ."

That's my cue to interrupt and force the issue. "I tell you what, why don't you assign me a local human-interest story and I'll write it up on spec. If you don't think it fits the style for your paper, we'll call it even. Sound good?" I grabbed a term from the film industry and I hope "spec" means the same thing to journalists. Basically, you write for the health of it and if somebody buys it—hooray.

Blink. Blink. Blink.

"What do you say? Should we give it a try? Just one local human-interest story."

"I guess it wouldn't hurt—"

That sounds like a "yes," people. That's all I need. "Thank you, Mr. Knudsen. You won't be sorry." I'm not sure why I said that last bit, but it sounds like something a cub reporter would say. I exit with a flourish before Mr. Knudsen can change his mind. And now I'm off to the sheriff's station for the *coup de grâce*.

The front desk is empty, so Furious Monkeys is either out sick or on a coffee break. I decide to try my luck with inviting myself directly back to Erick's office.

"Who'd you kill this time?" Deputy Paulsen has one plump hand on her gun and the other holds a toothpick that is picking lord knows what out of her teeth.

"Hilarious. I'm actually doing your job again. Maybe you'd like to accompany me to Erick's office and hear what a real investigation sounds like?"

"One day, Moon. That lip—"

I push past her, but she falls in directly behind me and seems to be taking me up on my offer. I never know when to quit. I was actually hoping for some alone time with Erick. I grin and pick up the pace.

However, I'm stopped short as I come around the corner and see who's sitting in the chair opposite the sheriff. Unfortunately, my quick stop results in Deputy Paulsen smacking into me as though we're a *Three Stooges* outtake.

Erick chuckles. "I'll take it from here, Paulsen." He waves her back to wherever she came from. Bully School, I'm guessing.

"Good morning, Miss Moon. You're up early."

"It happens every once in a while. How's your morning, Erick?"

He shakes his head and shrugs. "Have you met Quince Knudsen, the photographer over at the post?" He gestures to the boy sitting on the other side of his desk.

I shake my head and hope to goodness that my bribe served its purpose. "Don't think I've had the pleasure." I lean forward and reach out my hand. "Hi, Quince, I'm Mitzy."

Quince fumbles the handshake and says something like, "Hey."

I pull my hand back and make eye contact with Erick. I tilt my head meaningfully and ask, "You got a minute?"

"Yeah, we're just finishing up." He hands a business card to Quince. "You give this to Donna Jo and tell her I'm the reason you're late. Got it?"

Quince takes the card, nods, and slips past me out of the office.

I have to admit the kid is good. Apparently he didn't crack under interrogation. Nice to know. I drop into the recently vacated chair and lean back to get a better view of Erick.

"What brings you in this morning?"

"Well, Erick, I have a lead on the vehicle that hit Doc Ledo."

He leans forward and grins. "I can't wait to hear this one. A crime with no eyewitnesses and you suddenly know who was driving the car. Please, Moon, enlighten me."

I don't think I like his tone. "First of all, as I mentioned to you previously, there was a witness.

Whoever stole the angel statue saw the accident. So it stands—"

Erick holds up one finger to halt my word vomit. "About that. I got a very strange call from Olga Jorgensen this morning. She said that God saw fit to give her a miracle and this morning she woke up to find that statue back on her porch. You wouldn't happen to know anything about that, would you?"

I shrug and avoid his penetrating gaze. "The truck that hit Doc was a 1980 blue-and-white Chevy pickup, lifted. But that's not the strange part."

I see a faint hint of recognition in Erick's eyes, which I assume means he already knows who was driving the vehicle. But I continue to spin my tale. "Doc Ledo wasn't actually struck down on Pin Cherry Lane. My source tells me that he saw the truck back up to the spot where the body was found, take Doc Ledo out of the bed of the truck, and position him on the street where Artie found him. My source also says the driver of the vehicle even went so far as to put Doc Ledo's boots in the snow on the edge of the street."

"Well that sounds insane. Who told you this tale?"

"Think about it, Erick. The last thing Ledo remembers was searching for the right 'walking home' music on his phone. Wouldn't he do that as he was leaving the clinic? Not after he'd already walked five or six blocks through The Pines? Clearly whoever ran him down, hit him over on Gunnison Avenue. Then for some reason, known only to them, they loaded him in the back of their truck, drove over to Pin Cherry Lane and staged an accident there. I'm not saying it makes sense, I'm just telling you what my source reported."

Erick leans forward and fixes me with the intimidating stare I'd been working so hard to avoid. "I'll ask you again, Moon, where did you hear the story?"

Here goes nothing. "I'm sorry, Erick, but I can't reveal my sources."

"Nice try, Moon. I'm sure even you realize that protecting a source only applies to journalists." He leans back and rubs his freshly shaven chin. "You can tell me now, or I can charge you with accessory after the fact. Your choice."

"Well that's the thing, Erick. It's all part of a human-interest story I'm doing for the *Post*. So I do have the protection of the fourth estate and I am going to have to protect my sources. You have what you need." I stand and repeat my intel. "1980 blue-and-white Chevy pickup. Silas will be in contact later to see if you've tracked down the driver." I walk toward the door, feeling every one of my heartbeats as though it is a giant kettledrum in an orchestra.

Erick stands, swallows the distance between us in two easy strides, and grasps my arm. "This isn't over."

I've really only got the one tool left in my tool belt, so I step toward him and lean in close as I whisper, "I was hoping you'd say that, Erick."

He immediately drops my arm, mutters something, and stumbles backward.

I leave him sitting on the edge of his desk, flustered, and hopefully wanting more. Let's be clear—more of me, not more information.

I hightail it out of the sheriff's office and straight over to the hospital to update Ledo on my progress.

CHAPTER 19

AFTER A SURPRISINGLY UPBEAT visit with Ledo, I take my overworked hind end to Myrtle's Diner for a well-deserved lunch.

I barely finish stamping the snow off my boots before Tally shouts a happy greeting. "Hey, Mitzy. Coffee or cocoa?"

I take a seat at the counter and ponder my options. "I could use another cup of coffee."

"You betcha." Tally scurries around filling my beverage order.

Odell gives me the ol' spatula salute, and the welcome sizzle of the deep fryer lets me know heaven is on its way.

I grab the abandoned newspaper from the stool next to me and smile when I see the photos of all the flower arrangements at the pet cemetery. Quince did a fantastic job. Even in black and white the arrangements all look beautiful and would surely bring a smile to anyone's face.

"That was a good thing you done." Odell nods toward the paper.

"All I did was make a phone call. It's Doc Ledo that's the real hero around here. In fact, I just came from the hospital."

Tally's hand shakes and she spills a little coffee as she sets down my mug. "Everything okay?"

"He's doing great. When I got there he was just finishing up a meeting with the veterinarian from Broken Rock who's covering for him twice a week, and a traveling veterinarian who's going to cover the office three days a week and handle his house-calls for the livestock clients."

Tally nods and tries to put on a brave face. "Any break in the case?"

"Oh, yes. A big break. I feel like I've told the story so many times that everyone knows. But let me get you up to speed." I give them the extremely shortened version of the eyewitness statement and a description of the vehicle that's been identified.

Odell shakes his head and immediately busies himself with flipping burgers. I have a feeling, much like with Erick, that Odell knows who the driver might be.

"Did the sheriff make an arrest? Are they charging that maniac with attempted murder?" Tally is on the verge of tears.

"Silas is digging into it for me. Hopefully they'll make an arrest this afternoon. Seems like a pretty unique vehicle. But Ledo doesn't want to press charges."

Tally slams the coffee pot on the counter so hard I flinch from the expectation of showering glass. Somehow the amazing pot holds up and I'm spared any injury.

"Why in the H-E-double-hockey-sticks would he not want to press charges?" Tally spins around and marches to the telephone.

I would not want to be Ledo right now. I see her punching the buttons on that wall phone with a vengeance and I can only imagine the ear full of lecture that poor man is about to receive.

Odell sets my plate down and speaks in a low tone. "Come on out back when you're finished."

"You got it." I hope I'm not in trouble, but for now I'm going to enjoy these miraculous fries.

I decide to take an unprecedented approach to my lunch and eat slowly, while I continue reading the paper. I'm definitely impressed with the quality of the photographs. Although the article on page seven, about the Eagles home basketball game, wraps around a fairly blurry picture of the cheer-

leading squad. Well, I guess they can't all be win-
ners, Quince. Then I notice who's perched at the
top of the pyramid—queen of mean, Brynley—and I
chuckle. I'd have to say Quince pulled this shot out
of focus on purpose rather than accident. I'm liking
this kid more and more every day.

I savor the last of my french fries as I read the
article about a local philanthropist's generous donation to the Pin Cherry Harbor High School. The
obligatory picture of me holding a giant check and
shaking the principal's hand nearly makes me spit
take my coffee. I look so grown up. Almost like I
know what I'm doing. Maybe I should've been an
actress? Although, most of what I'm doing seems
like I'm making it up as I go along. Maybe improv?

"You about done out there? Somethin' wrong
with the food? Never seen ya eat this slow in my
life." Odell laughs heartily.

"I was trying on some manners for size. Apparently they don't fit." We share a laugh as I lick the
salt off my fingers and wipe my mouth with the thin
paper napkin.

I bus my dishes and slip them in the tub behind
the counter before I follow Odell out the back door.
He takes the ragged cigarette from his shirt pocket,
pinches it between his lips, and collects his
thoughts.

I stare at that worn nicotine stick and smile. It's just so like Odell to prove to himself every day that he's still strong enough. According to him, he quit smoking fifteen years ago and just keeps the cigarette around like a badge of honor. Anyway, he must've had something to tell me. "So, what's going on?"

"I'm sure Harper will come to the same conclusion as me, but I'm pretty sure that truck you're describing belongs to Johan Olafsson."

Why does that name sound so familiar? Oh right, Deputy Paulsen's nemesis. "I've never seen Johan drive anything but a tractor."

Odell nods solemnly. "Yep. Given he's a bit of a drinker, and between the bartender making him weak drinks and the tractor not goin' more than twenty-five miles an hour, it seemed like a pretty good arrangement for everyone involved. But winter isn't really tractor weather, and it sounds like Johan mighta pulled a fast one on the bartender. Did your witness get a look at the driver?"

"Yeah, but I just reported the information about the vehicle and the staging of the accident." I lower my voice and look around. "Don't mention anything to Tally."

Odell pulls the cigarette from the corner of his mouth and slides it purposefully into the pocket of his faded denim shirt. "What do you mean 'staging' of the accident?"

I proceed to tell him the far-fetched tale of the driver coming down the street, backing up to the precise location across from The Pines, and placing the body on the street.

Odell shakes his head. "I've heard some strange things in my day, but that takes the cake."

"Right? Why would someone who plans to flee the scene of an accident take the time to move the body from Gunnison over to Pin Cherry Lane? And then leave? It makes no sense to me."

"Are you sure the accident happened on Gunnison?"

"I'm only guessing because of what Ledo said about his music. But they clearly moved the body from somewhere."

"Right under that big streetlight on the corner of Spruce and Pin Cherry, right?"

"Yup. That's where Artie pointed on her map of the city streets."

"She always plows The Pines first," mumbles Odell.

Something about that tickles a memory. Think, Mitzy, think. What was it that Artie said? Ah ha! "Except that night she didn't."

"What do you mean?"

"Well, she told me not to say anything, but Artie plowed the streets over by the park first, so everyone could get to the Extravaganza. Then she went around, plowed Gunnison, and came in to The Pines from the far side. Not her usual route."

Odell runs a hand through his grey buzz cut and nods his head slowly. "So if Toledo was hit on Gunnison and the driver knew Artie's route . . . Seems like he moved the doc's body so it would be discovered sooner."

"So you're saying this guy, Johan, has a conscience?"

"Of course. Just because he drinks too much once in a while doesn't mean he hasn't got a heart of gold."

A moment of silence hangs between us and I know we're both thinking about my grandmother and the way her drinking problem tore apart her relationship with Odell—despite the fact that she also has a heart of gold.

"Maybe that's why Ledo doesn't want to press charges?"

"If Sheriff Harper goes for a felony, it won't matter what Doc Ledo wants."

"Then I guess I'd better keep digging. Since my client wouldn't want that to happen."

"You're a good kid, Mitzy. Let's keep this just

between us." Odell pats me on the shoulder and leads the way back inside.

"Mmhmm." Just between me and Odell—and Grams, and Silas.

I'm so amped up I can't possibly wait until I get back to the bookstore. I pull out my phone to call Silas as I'm rushing down the sidewalk.

CRASH!

I fall backward onto the salt-covered sidewalk and my phone flies into a snowbank.

"Mitzy!" Strong arms scoop me up and set me on my feet.

However, I stop the extending hand before it can complete its mission to brush the snow off my behind. "I can handle that part." I brush off the snow and look up into the concerned face of Rory Bombay.

"Are you all right? I was gazing up at the trail that airplane was leaving and the way the sun was illuminating— Anyway, I was distracted and I can't apologize enough for crashing into you. Are you sure you're not hurt?"

I have absolutely no intention of telling Rory how many times I've bounced off my ample back-side, but I also don't have time for a pity party. "I'm fine. Honestly, I'm just fine. I really have to get back to the bookshop."

"Let me escort you. Just to make sure there's no further incident."

"Oh, don't worry about it. Excuse me. I need to get my phone. I slide past him and begin digging through the mound of snow left by whoever shoveled the sidewalk. I hope I'm actually searching around the approximate trajectory that my phone took. The snow clings to my mittens, and, as it starts to melt, the frigid water almost burns my skin with cold.

A firm hand grips my shoulder. "Allow me. You'll get frostbite with those thin woolen mittens. Really, it's the least I can do." Rory pulls me to my feet and drops down on one knee to take over my search.

I want to blurt out that his stupid ring almost killed me. But I just can't seem to square the two things in my mind. A diabolical man giving me some kind of magically poisoned ring doesn't reconcile with the kind gentleman down on his knees in the dirty street snow digging for my phone. Especially not when I'm the one who wasn't paying attention because I was messing with my—Oh my gosh! Ledo's phone! That's it!

"Ah, here it is, Miss Moon." Rory stands, wipes off my phone on his pants, and hands it to me as though it were a priceless bottle of wine.

"Thanks. I gotta go, but thanks." I break into an

uncharacteristic jog and head down the alleyway to one of my garages. Next stop, Gunnison Avenue.

As I drive toward the veterinary clinic, I make a desperate plea to my mood ring.

"Look, I don't really understand how you work or even why you work, but I really need to find Toledo's phone and I really need your help. So, I'm going to get out there and dig my little fingers within an inch of their life and I need you to point them in the right direction. Deal?"

I hold my breath as I wait for the smallest flicker of a sign from my moody mood ring. The irony is not lost on me.

No sign is forthcoming.

I pull into the parking lot of the clinic and walk to the front door. Then I make a one-hundred-and-eighty-degree turn and walk slowly toward the street. As I approach Gunnison Avenue, I look for any signs that may possibly remain to indicate there was an accident.

I'm reasonably sure that the plow came down the road after Doc Ledo was struck. The prospect of digging through three or four feet of icy snow-bank to try to find his phone does not entice.

I walk back and forth in front of the clinic, struggling to come up with a better plan.

A lovely young woman with a rambunctious Siberian husky approaches from the parking lot.

"Are you waiting for your fur baby?"

I suppose I do look like an anxious parent waiting to hear if I've had triplets or quadruplets. "No, thanks though." Inspiration strikes. "I slipped and my phone flew out of my hand and went into the snowbank. I was just trying to work up the courage to start digging for it.

She laughs uproariously and slaps her thigh.

I'm about to give her a piece of my mind concerning how rude it is to laugh at someone's misfortune when she drops some knowledge on me.

"Well today is your lucky day. Mistletoe is the best darn digger this side of the Arctic Circle. You point her in a direction and she'll dig clear to China."

I suppress the need to tell her that you can't actually dig to China, and pledge to let that childhood myth remain. Now, if I can just get a tiny bit of cooperation from my ring.

"Oh my gosh! That's the best news I've had all day. Let me retrace my steps and see if I can at least narrow down the area for little Mistletoe. And then we'll just let her dig, right?"

The lady nods her head. She hunkers down to give Mistletoe a pep talk, and I whisper some encouraging words to my ring.

Stepping off the curb, roughly where I imagine Toledo took his last step, I try to visualize the blue-

and-white truck impacting me on the left side. If Ledo was holding his phone— And then the vision hits me. I feel the impact. I see the phone fly out of my hand, so high in the air . . . I can feel my body hurtle through space and slam into the street. And my phone . . . My phone lands all the way in the opposing lane of traffic. I bend over and place my hands on my knees as I struggle to catch my breath. The imagery was so vivid, and the feelings so real, I'm a little bit dizzy.

"Hey, are you okay?"

"Oh yeah. I guess I'm probably coming down with something. I'm sorry. I think my phone is over there." I point across the street.

She looks at me like I might be a little crazy.

By my calculations, if Toledo's phone landed in the lane of oncoming traffic it's pretty likely that Artie plowed it into the snowbank across the street when she came up Gunnison from plowing the area around the park.

"All right. Come on, Mistletoe, let's go find this phone."

I have to admire this lady's belief in her puppers.

We check traffic and jog across the street.

My left ring finger tugs toward the embankment. Finally! Some help from my ring. My hand pulls toward the snowbank as I move it back and forth like a dowsing rod. I feel heat increase as I move to the right.

Mistletoe follows so closely I'm starting to wonder if she can sense the heat from the ring?

"Right here. I think this is where it landed."

To the lady's credit, she seems to believe me and not think that I'm completely insane. She let's Mistletoe off-leash. "Dig deep, Missy. Dig deep," she encourages the husky.

I cannot believe my eyes as I watch this Tasmanian devil-dog dig into the snowbank like it contains the juiciest pile of treats a dog could ever imagine. Mistletoe rears up on her back legs, pounces down with her two front paws together and digs like a mad dog. I stupidly reach for my actual phone in my pocket, because I really want to film this anomaly. Thankfully, a moment of lucidity stops me from pulling out the very phone she's supposedly digging for, and I instead join the chant. "Dig deep, Missy. Dig deep."

Less than thirty seconds later, that magnificent beast has nearly disappeared into the snowbank.

Mistletoe's owner looks at me and smiles. "She's amazing isn't she?"

I nod fervently. "She's incredible."

Suddenly the digging stops.

"What is it, Missy? You got that phone, Missy?"

Here's the moment of truth. Is this lady absolutely bonkers? Is her dog going to back out of that hole with nothing more than a cold muzzle?

Mistletoe reverses out of the snow-tunnel, and to my utter shock, is holding a cell phone gently in her mouth.

"Holy mackerel." I crouch down and hold out my hand. Mistletoe walks over and drops the phone in my hand like it's a tennis ball and we've been playing this game for hours.

Mistletoe's owner pulls some treats from the pocket of her winter coat and hands what looks like a delicious strip of beef jerky to the husky.

"Thank you so much! You have no idea—"

"Oh, think nothing of it. You made Mistletoe's day. She just loves to dig."

"Well, I can't thank you enough. But, if you wouldn't mind, I'd like to do a story on you and Mistletoe for the *Post*. I'm a freelance reporter and I just think it would make a great feel-good piece for this week's edition."

I lean down and pat Mistletoe profusely. "What do you say? A nice little human-interest story to lift everyone's holiday spirits?"

"Oh, what the heck."

I follow her inside the clinic to get a piece of paper and write down all of the particulars, because thank goodness the phone we recovered from the snowbank is dead, giving me the perfect excuse not to be able to tap out some notes on "my phone."

After we exchange the information, I give Mistletoe another pat of gratitude and make my escape before the receptionist asks the reason for my visit.

As I drive back to the bookstore, I call Silas. Where to begin . . .

CHAPTER 20

ON MY WAY back to the Bell, Book & Candle, I can't help but wonder if Silas will be able to get to Johan before Erick. I don't actually agree with Ledo's decision not to press charges, but I'm extremely curious to know why Mr. Olafsson moved the body. Part of me even worries that moving the body caused more serious injury than the initial impact. However, after the sensory overload of imagery that I was forced to relive in front of the veterinary clinic, I can't imagine anything worse than the impact.

Oh, *Little Rascals*. I missed my turn. With a quick check in the rearview, I back up, and slip down the alley.

After I close the garage door, but before I'm safely inside, Mr. Bombay appears in the alley.

"This is the second time today, Rory. I'm thinking it can't be an accident."

"You found me out. I was hoping you'd allow me to take you out for a slice of pie and some coffee this afternoon. I enjoyed our lunch together and I thought perhaps we needed one more engagement before you'd to agree to dinner."

I definitely want to confront him about the ring, but if he has an evil master plan I don't think I want to learn about it in this alley. A public place seems like a safer bet. And a public place where I know someone's got my back seems even safer. "I will agree on two conditions."

Rory bows. "Agreed. Name your conditions."

"First of all, you agree to answer any and all of my questions, honestly. Nothing is off limits. Nothing is placed on hold."

Rory's eyes darken, but he nods his agreement. "And the second condition?"

"That you admit here and now that you lied about the pin cherry pie at Myrtle's Diner. I want you to acknowledge that you repeated unverified gossip, because I know for a fact that Odell makes his own pie from a family recipe."

Rory chuckles warmly. "You got me. The owner of the patisserie is a bit of a gossip, and I took her at her word without bothering to check the facts. I acquiesce."

I grin smugly. "Good. Now let's go to Myrtle's Diner and have a slice of Pin Cherry Harbor's best pin cherry pie."

He offers me his elbow, which I take.

"Would you say it's too cold for pie à la mode?"

I laugh openly. "Never."

Tucked into a squeaky-clean booth at the diner, Rory orders us two slices of pin cherry pie à la mode and two cups of coffee.

"Would you excuse me for one moment?"

I nod, and he gets up and walks to the counter. "Pardon me, Odell?"

Odell looks up without the characteristic warmth in his eyes and nods.

"I owe you an apology, sir. I unwittingly repeated some gossip and I apologize for impugning your reputation." Rory nods.

Odell shrugs and mumbles his thanks.

Rory returns to the booth, sits down, and looks at me with an adorable plea in his green eyes. "Enough penance, Miss Moon?"

I try to ignore the warm tingle in my tummy. "For today."

He slides his hand across the table and strokes the back of my hand.

Unfortunately, the gesture reminds me of what I really need to ask him about. I lean back and put both my hands in my lap. Resting the left on top so that a casual glance down will show me any message I might be lucky enough to get from my ring.

"You're not wearing the ring I gave you. Did you not like it?"

I toy with the idea of making up a story about being allergic to the metal, but that wouldn't give me the answers I need. On the other hand, I can hardly tell him the truth about my psychic powers, so I attempt to split the difference. "I had a strange reaction to the ring and Silas told me I shouldn't wear it."

Rory clenches his jaw, and I can see him weighing his own options. "What type of reaction?"

Touché. Perhaps he's better at this game than I am. "It's a little hard to describe. Maybe it was an allergy, but I definitely felt unwell." That's as near as I can come to the truth, and I hope it's enough to get me an answer.

"My apologies." He takes a deep breath and mumbles, "I should've known."

I lean forward. "Should've known what?"

He stares at me with a hint of intrigue lighting his gaze. "I suppose I wasn't entirely honest."

I knew it. Well, Silas knew it, but we knew it.

"I didn't get the ring at an estate sale. I fabricated that bit, because I didn't want you to refuse the gift. I assumed that if you knew I'd spent a tidy sum on it you would feel undue obligation. And I

216 / TRIXIE SILVERTALE

honestly thought it was a beautiful ring and didn't intend it to mean more than what it was—a friendly gift."

"All right. So what is it that you should've known?"

"The woman I bought it from has somewhat of a reputation in this town."

If he's about to tell me there's some version of *The Best Little Whorehouse in Texas* in Pin Cherry Harbor, I will eat my hat. And for only the second time in my life I'm actually wearing a hat, so the possibility is quite real. "A woman of ill repute?"

Rory laughs a little too long at my expense. "You are the most refreshing combination of brilliance and humor, and of course beauty. But let me get back to my story."

Odell sets our plates on the table with one hand and somehow manages to add two cups of coffee to the spread with the other. The man has skills.

"Thanks, Odell. I'm really looking forward to this." I wink.

He shrugs and heads back into the kitchen.

All right. He doesn't like Mr. Bombay. Is there a secret club I don't know about? Do they have jackets? I take a bite of golden, flaky crust, with delicious just-sweet-enough filling, and melty ice cream oozing over it all, and I forgive Odell all of his sins.

"You were right about the pie, Mitzy. It is the

best." Rory scoops a forkful of his own sinful slice and leans across the table to feed it to me.

My cheeks flush, but I'm no fool. I take the bite. "So tell me about this woman."

"Ah, yes. Ania Karina Nowak. A Polish gypsy who has a palm reading and tarot shop on the outskirts of town."

"How scandalous. That can't go over well with the locals."

"Indeed. It would appear that your grandmother was one of the leaders of the group that got the shop closed down, temporarily. I always heard about their decades-long feud, but I didn't think much of it, until today."

"What do you mean?"

"I bought the ring from Ania. I may have made the mistake of mentioning for whom the ring was intended. She no doubt made the connection between 'new owner of the bookshop' and the rumors about Isadora's heir."

Wow, seems like Grams really held some sway in this town. "What are you saying?"

"I know you're going to think it sounds crazy, but perhaps Ania put a gypsy curse on the ring. Terribly sorry. Perhaps I can take it back to her and convince her to remove the curse."

I swallow my delicious pie, but it feels a little like sand in my throat. Psychic powers. Alchemy.

Gypsy curses. Where does it end? And why does it sound like Rory believes that a Gypsy curse is real?

"I'm sure you're wondering why I would believe in a Gypsy curse." He chuckles. "My mother was very superstitious. I'm sure I grew up believing a lot of things that other people would find foolish. I throw salt over my left shoulder if I spill it. If I drop a knife, I know a man is coming to visit. If I see a penny, I pick it up. Mostly silly things that others ignore."

I take another bite of pie and toy with my next move. "Is Bombay your real name?"

He smiles a smile that could melt an igloo in two minutes flat.

I tear my eyes away and gulp down some coffee to cover my discomfort.

"It is. Happy to show you my driver's license, if that helps."

"No need. It's not like Mizithra is a common name. I get it." I lift my mug, but before I can take another sip of my coffee, he reaches across the table and wipes the tip of my chin with his thumb.

"You had a little ice cream there."

Oh boy, red flags, sirens, tingles. He's just too good to be true.

"Miss Moon, I'm afraid I need you to come down to the station. I had another conversation with Quince Knudsen and he let it slip that he'd met you before that day in my office." Erick raises a suspicious eyebrow and stares knowingly.

Wait? What? I didn't hear the door open. There was certainly no indication on Rory's face that Erick was approaching. This can't be happening. The man is immune to my advances and yet he seems to do everything in his power to make sure no one else accepts them either. I'm just about to un-leash some choice words when Rory beats me to the punch.

"Tell you what, Sheriff Harper. As soon as Mitzy and I finish our pie, I'll escort her over to the station. I assume you're asking her to come in volun-tarily and not officially, correct?"

Erick crosses his well-muscled arms over his broad chest and I blush a little. "Cooperation would be her best option at this point, Mr. Bombay."

"Very well, we'll see you shortly." The dismis-sive tone in Rory's voice is admirable.

Erick turns his baby blues on me and adds very officially, "See you shortly, Moon." He saunters out of the diner and it takes every ounce of self-control I possess not to turn and look over my shoulder.

Rory's hand reaches across the table and grasps my fingers. "Is there something I should know about you and Sheriff Harper?"

As far as I know, there's absolutely nothing he should know about Sheriff Harper and me. I suppose a humorous answer would be the best thing to diffuse the situation. "Only that he's accused me of murder twice since I've moved to this town."

Rory chuckles. "That's not exactly what I meant, but it's good to know."

CHAPTER 21

I FEEL A LITTLE GUILTY about ducking out on Erick's summons and sneaking back to the Bell, Book & Candle, but there's no way I'm going into the station without Silas. Lucky for me, my alchemist-attorney is engaged in a pantomime game of charades with Grams.

"I am so glad to see the two of you," I exclaim as the bookcase slides closed. "I've had the weirdest day!"

Silas nods and Grams glares at me.

"Oh, sorry. Did you guys need an interpreter?"

"Well, what do you think, young lady?" Grams rests her ghostly fists on her hips. "Silas has just informed me that the emerald ring you accepted from Rory Bombay is cursed!" She shoots up to the ceiling like a phantom rocket and clucks her tongue with worry.

Silas straightens his faded green bowtie and harrumphs into his mustache. "I believe she was attempting to convince me to formulate some fashion of retaliation against Mr. Bombay."

Ghost-ma torpedoes from the ceiling, straight through me as she hollers, "You're darn tootin'!"

"Wow. You two really got into it while I was— away." Now seems like the wrong time to tell them that I was having pie and ice cream with— Oops, almost sold myself out.

"With who?" Grams floats in front of my face with a heap of otherworldly vengeance oozing from her aura.

"With whom," I correct.

"Why you little . . ."

Ignoring Grams' tantrum, I address the room. "I have several very interesting pieces of information to share, and if Grams can calm down for one second, I think I can clear up this whole mess."

Silas gazes through his enchanted spectacles and locates Grams. "Isadora, I believe we owe it to Mitzy to hear her side of things before we select a course of action."

Grams vanishes into the wall and I take that as further protest, but choose to soldier on. By the time

I'm halfway into the story of Mistletoe and the missing phone, Grams materializes behind Silas.

"Do you mean to tell me that you recovered Doctor Toledo's cellular phone from a snowbank on Gunnison Avenue?"

I nod triumphantly. "That is exactly what I'm telling you, and can you believe how my ring was working like a homing beacon?"

"I would postulate that your explanation would indicate that a dowsing rod is a more accurate description, but either way it is an impressive find. You will have to turn the cellular phone in to the sheriff and make a formal statement."

"Yeah, Erick came into the diner and asked me to stop by the station. Well, it was more like a demand, but I didn't want to go in until I brought you guys up to speed."

"I will place a call on your behalf and attempt to buy us a few days respite from the Sheriff's summons." Silas strokes his mustache and wags his head.

"Any luck getting a hold of Johan?"

"His daughter was house sitting for him, with her three offspring. She said he and Marguerite were in Canada."

"That seems sketchy. Did she say why?"

"She did not." Silas removes the wire-rimmed

glasses. "What does 'sketchy' have to do with travel?"

"Sketchy just means that it seems shady, like not on the up-and-up. I mean, do you think he's running from the law?"

"She agreed to pass along my message, so perhaps we will have a better understanding once we talk to Mr. Olafsson."

Grams can no longer keep silent. "And what does this phone recovery have to do with that wicked Mr. Bombay?"

"Oh, I forgot all about the Polish gypsy!"

Grams immediately avoids eye contact and Silas shakes his head. I share the story of the ring and make every effort to lift all blame from Rory's shoulders as I paint the picture of a vindictive, wronged gypsy.

"I was hoping to avoid this discussion, Mitzy. However, I fear I must be the one to inform you that your grandmother made her fair share of enemies in her lifetime. Not the least of which was the Polish gypsy woman who resides on the outskirts of town, Ania Karina Nowak."

My head is swimming with thoughts, ideas, and concerns. "And you think this Polish gypsy woman somehow knows about my gifts? Why else would she curse a ring in a specific way that would overload my psychic powers and make me sick?"

"Your grandmother and this woman didn't see eye to eye about all things clairvoyant. Isadora thought this woman to be a fraud and said as much, quite publicly."

"Meaning?"

"I believe the sheriff, at the time, took punitive action and the gypsy woman was forced to close her palm-reading shop, at least temporarily."

Grams materializes next to Silas. "She was bilking money from people who couldn't afford it. I'm telling you, I did this community a favor. Tell him what I said, Mitzy. Tell him."

I relay her message to Silas and he slips his magicked spectacles from his pocket and puts them on. "My dear Isadora, there are perhaps at least two sides to each tale. You can hardly expect your granddaughter to make a judicious choice with only half a story."

"Half a story! Half the story was all that Polish witch ever gave. It makes perfect sense that she would be selling half-baked curses! She's probably already opened another business and she's just looking for more ways to bamboozle hard-working citizens."

"So you don't think this has anything to do with me?"

Silas shakes his head slowly and his saggy jowls jostle back and forth. "I would suspect that this woman indeed knowingly cursed the ring before selling it to Mr. Bombay. She would have every reason to strike back at something Isadora holds dear."

"How would she—"

"If she has knowledge of your relation to Isadora, perhaps she merely suspects you possess a gift. Conceivably this cursed ring was merely a test. You must inform Rory to keep your reaction from the woman. The last thing we want to do is confirm her suspicions."

"The ring? Can you uncurse it or something?"

"I will endeavor to discern the mechanism of the curse and postulate a disruption. However, it is possible that you will not be able to wear the ring."

"You mean, ever?"

"Indeed." Silas's phone rings and interrupts our bizarre debate.

"Good afternoon. Silas Willoughby speaking. How may I be of assistance?"

Yikes, he really takes manners to the next level.

"You could learn a thing or two from him, young lady."

"Listen, Grams, I don't know what you've got against Rory, but once again he's innocent of your accusations. I really think you need to give him another chance. People change."

Grams rolls her eyes and dematerializes.

I open my mouth to scold her, but Silas interrupts.

"Mr. Olafsson has returned from Canada. I suggest we head over to the farm at once. It won't take long for Sheriff Harper to catch wind of their arrival."

CHAPTER 22

THE ONLY CONVERSATION on the way out to the Olafsson farm is the monotony of Silas giving me directions. When I pull up in front of an efficient, white, two-story farmhouse, Silas reaches over and places his hand on top of mine on the steering wheel.

"I should like to do most of the talking, do you understand?"

I really don't understand. But I do get the feeling that Silas has a subtlety that I lack. "All right. Whatever you say."

"Thank you." We trudge through the freshly shoveled path, climb the steps, and knock on the front door.

The man who answers looks decades older than

the man I remember seeing on the tractor driving down Main Street.

Silas extends his hand. "Thank you for seeing us, Johan."

Mr. Olafsson weakly shakes my attorney's outstretched hand and invites us into the living room. He offers us neither refreshment nor seats as he collapses into a recliner.

"May we sit down, Johan?"

The man in the chair looks up at us as though he's unsure how we got into his house. "What? Oh, of course. Yes, have a seat." He leans forward with his elbows on his knees and runs his hands through his hair, haphazardly attempting to smooth it into place.

"We're sorry to have bothered you so late in the day. How's Marguerite?"

The hollow-eyed stare that peers out at Silas and me is haunting and heartbreaking. My mood ring shifts to darkest blue and my stomach tightens in preparation for what I know is going to be horrible news.

"She's not well. She's not well at all. She's got six more of them radiation treatments before they can even tell us if they're working. We keep drivin' over to Montreal to that there proton beam machine. But all it seems to be doing so far is wearing her down.

It's almost like she's sicker now than before we started the treatments." He leans back in the chair and sighs heavily—the sound of a broken man who's holding his family together with a thread of hope stretched so thin, it could snap at any moment.

Silas nods and looks at me out of the corner of his eye.

"I'm so sorry to hear that, Johan. Marguerite has always been a kind woman and I do hope the very best for her, and your family. Is there anything we can do?"

Johan stares blankly at both of us. It's clear the weight of his wife's illness has pushed him near to breaking. He says nothing.

"I hesitate to put any more on your plate, but I feel you should know that the sheriff will most likely pay you a visit this evening or first thing in the morning."

The look in Johan's eyes speaks volumes. It's not the wild, panicked look of a cornered animal, it's the look of a man who's just one burden away from giving up.

Silas takes a deep breath and continues, "An eyewitness has come forward and identified the vehicle that struck down Doc Ledo."

Johan nods but doesn't speak or show any emotion.

"The story we heard is that the doctor was

struck by a blue-and-white 1980 Chevy pickup truck on Gunnison Avenue in front of the clinic."

This information does get a reaction from our host. He leans forward and swallows before his fingers grip the arms of the chair so hard his knuckles turn white.

"And believe it or not, the eyewitness says the driver of the vehicle then moved the doctor's body over to where it was actually discovered on Pin Cherry Lane."

I admire the way Silas seamlessly blends the actual eyewitness stuff with the "from Mitzy's psychic visions" stuff.

Johan slowly shakes his head and his shoulders slump forward.

"The driver must've had a good reason." Silas pauses, and the distant ticking of a clock resounds like a gong in the silence. "If there's any way I can help you, I will. Can you tell us what happened?"

The soft, encouraging timbre of Silas's voice nearly forces me to confess to a crime I didn't commit.

Johan wrings his hands two or three times as he stares fixedly at the floor. "I don't know how much the two of you know about getting old or about medical insurance, but neither one of them is anything like it's cracked up to be. Insurance don't seem to cover nothing, and gettin' old happens faster than you ever thought it would. When Marguerite got sick, we figured she'd take a few pills, maybe have to slow down a little, and that would be that. But when the tests came back, they told us she had some rare form of brain cancer that could only be treated with this special machine they got down at the Mayo Clinic. Well, we thought that was the worst news we'd ever heard."

"That must've been tough on both of you."

"That wasn't even the tough part. Tough part came when the insurance company said they wouldn't cover the proton therapy treatments because the provider was outside our network and somethin' about experimental treatments. You get the idea. Only one cure. Big expensive treatment. Insurance ain't gonna pay. So, seein' as how Marguerite is French-Canadian, with dual citizenship and what not, we figured we'd head up to Canada and take advantage of that socialist medicine. So, the treatments are every two weeks and it's an eighteen-hour drive, one way, to the only facility in Canada."

Silas nods. "That must be very difficult for her when she's feeling so ill."

I shake my head silently, unable to add anything meaningful to the conversation.

Johan takes a ragged breath and finally looks up from the floor. His eyes plead for understanding.

"He just stepped out right in front of me. You see, one minute he was standing on the curb looking at his phone, and the next—BAM! There was nothin' I coulda done."

"We know. We know." Silas waits a beat before asking, "But why didn't you call an ambulance?"

"Ah, you know me, Silas. I never know when to quit, always have one too many. Maybe I was driving too fast. Either way, you know they're gonna take my license. Then who's gonna drive Marguerite to her treatments?" His head falls into his hands and he mumbles, "Couldn't let 'em take my license. Couldn't let that happen." He wrings his hands and exhales long and slow. "I moved him over to Pin Cherry Lane so Artie would find him right away."

Despite Silas telling me to let him do all the talking, I can't take this any longer. I don't have the heart to tell Johan that Artie changed her route that night, but I have to do something. I kneel down next to Johan and place my hand on his knee. "Mr. Olafsson, I realize you don't really know me. But Doc Ledo is going to be paralyzed. And, in spite of that, he doesn't want to press charges. But if you sit here and wait for Erick to hunt you down, it's going to be bad. There's just no way out."

He sighs deeply.

"Johan, the best thing you can do is surrender

yourself to the sheriff. Get ahead of this thing, and let me help you. Like Mitzy said, the sheriff has the information about the vehicle. And if you wait for him to apprehend you, I'm afraid this whole thing could go sideways and then where will Marguerite be?"

"Maybe we just leave for Canada right now, and won't come back."

"Look, Mr. Olafsson, you seem like a good man. I don't see how you could live with yourself if you don't do the right thing. But I promise you, Silas will do everything he can to help you and—" I look at Silas and he nods for me to continue "—I will make sure that Marguerite doesn't miss a single treatment. All right?"

Silas mutters his agreement. "I recommend you call the sheriff before time runs out." He passes his phone to Johan.

The aging, brokenhearted farmer stares at the cell phone for a long time. And before he makes his decision, the soft shuffle of feet echoes from the hallway as Marguerite, head wrapped in a turban, dark circles under her eyes, enters the room.

Johan looks up with eyes full of love and admiration.

Marguerite smiles weakly. "My life—is not worth your soul. This too shall pass, my love."

He takes a hold of Silas's phone and presses "call."

I return to my place on the couch beside my amazing lawyer, and friend. Silas gives my knee a fatherly pat, and we both wait with bated breath while Mr. Olafsson tells his story to Sheriff Harper. By the time he's finished and hands the phone back to Silas, Marguerite has returned to bed, and the three of us are once again alone in the living room.

"He said if I come on down to the station to-morrow morning and turn myself in, it'll go a long way to making things right. He also said I should probably get a lawyer." Johan looks hopefully at Silas.

Silas chuckles lightly. "It goes without saying that you'll be well represented." He nods and rises from the couch.

I follow suit and Silas pats Johan firmly on the shoulder as we walk to the front door. "Shall we say 9:00 a.m. at the station?"

"Yes, sir."

As we're stepping out the front door, Johan calls meekly, "You'll tell Doc Ledo how sorry I am, won't you?"

I turn and nod. "Absolutely! I absolutely will."

CHAPTER 23

I AWAKEN to the silent predawn darkness and I know in my gut I won't be falling back asleep. I roll over to scratch Pyewacket, but his usual spot on the bed next to me is empty.

I whisper into the gloom, "Pye? Pyewacket, where are you?"

"Why are you whispering, dear?"

"*Robinson Crusoe!* Really, Grams, first thing in the morning? When I have a full bladder? You're not playing fair."

"Oh, Mitzy. You're too much."

I roll out of bed and stumble to the bathroom. I can't believe it, but there's absolutely no way I'm going to fall back asleep, and it's starting to feel like getting up early is becoming a habit. A terrible habit, which I intend breaking as soon as possible.

A ghostly chuckle drifts through the wall.

"You don't know me. I could become an early bird, you'll see."

"All right, whatever you say."

"So where's Pyewacket?"

"He went slinking out of here in the middle of the night and never returned. I didn't see any trouble, but he's been sitting by that back door like someone was paying him to be on watch duty."

My brain is far from its peak performance at this hour, but I know Pyewacket seldom does anything by accident. I dress quickly and rush downstairs. As promised, Pye is sitting in front of the back door on high alert.

"What are you up to?"

He turns and adds another row of claw marks to the well-scratched metal door.

I open it, thinking he means to take a morning run, but as soon as the frosty air hits his whiskers he bounds back into the bowels of the bookshop.

I'm about to slam the door against the cold when I notice an envelope wedged under a small box.

Opening the door a bit farther, I venture a peek up and down the alley.

Empty.

I snatch the box and envelope and hurry back

upstairs. I set both items on the coffee table and wait for Grams to appear.

"Who from?"

"I'm not sure. Pyewacket wasn't exactly forthcoming."

"What do you mean?"

"He scratched the back door, and when I opened it to let him out he ran back inside and I discovered this package."

"Is it from that horrible gypsy woman?" Grams arches a perfectly drawn brow.

"No idea. The envelope is blank and the box is pretty nondescript. Do you think I should open it?"

"I suppose . . ."

With my limited paranormal knowledge, I have a growing distrust for inexplicable items appearing out of thin air. I grab my phone, swipe up Silas's phone number, and instruct Grams, "If things go sideways when I open this up, you call Silas, all right?"

"I'll do my best, honey."

I start with the envelope, carefully sliding my finger under the flap, loosening the seal, and removing the note. "It looks like a man's handwriting."

"'Dearest Mitzy, I feel terrible about the cursed ring and I'd like to beg for your forgiveness. I would greatly appreciate an opportunity to make it up to you. Please allow me the pleasure of escorting you to dinner at Yves Bistro tomorrow night. The enclosed gift is yours to keep regardless of your answer, and it is most assuredly un-cursed! See you at breakfast, R.'"

Grams cracks off a long, low whistle. "That man is full of surprises and utterly relentless. I suppose you'll have to go to supper."

I set down the card and look at Grams with more shock than anything else. "Hold on a minute. Do you suddenly approve of Mr. Bombay? The terrible, horrible, no good, very bad man?"

Grams waves her bejeweled hand dismissively in my direction. "Never look a gift horse in the mouth, dear."

"I have no idea what that means, Grams. But it sounds to me like you're saying that your affections can be purchased."

I'm not sure if you've ever been chased by an angry ghost before, but they are very hard to out run. When I finally collapse onto the bed in a heap of giggles, Grams is laughing at least as hard as me.

She catches her breath first. Which I suppose is no surprise, since she's a ghost and really doesn't need the air. "Well, are you going to open that little box or not?"

"As you wish." I walk back to the coffee table, sit down in the scalloped-back chair, and carefully open the box. Inside, curled into a somehow perfect blooming rose, is a gorgeous pair of red, kidskin-leather winter gloves.

"The man has taste."

"And a flair for the romantic gesture."

I bring Grams up to speed on my horrible thin-wool-mittens-digging-through-the-snowbank incident and she fans herself with one hand. "Oh my, that is dashing."

"All right, Grams, enough girl talk. I gotta get some breakfast and get over to see Doc Ledo. I've decided that since Johan is turning himself in today, there's no reason for me to take Ledo's phone to the sheriff's station."

"Aren't you looking for an excuse to see Erick? Weighing your options?"

"Cut it out. In case you haven't noticed, there are no options to weigh. If we count all of the invitations to dinner I've received, the grand total is one."

"You know what they say, Mitzy, a bird in the hand is worth two in the bush."

"A stitch in time saves nine, don't cry over spilt milk, curiosity killed the cat?"

"REE-ow!" The sound of imminent retribution.

"Sorry, Pye! It was just a joke."

"Honestly! Just go to your breakfast." She chuckles under her breath.

"See you later, Grams. Love you." I glance over

my shoulder to give a wave and lo and behold ghost tears are pouring down my grandmother's face. "What is it? What did I say?"

"It's just—I love you too, sweetie."

Big girl emotions are not my strong suit, so I head out of the bookshop and over to the diner. The usual Friday morning crowd occupies the four-top by the front window and the booth in the back corner. My newspaper guy is sitting on one of the stools at the counter. I take a seat at the end of the counter and give Odell a nod. "I'll have the special, please"

He smiles and says, "What's the word?"

"Let's see . . . I solved the case—make that cases —I'm turning in my first story for the *Post* today, and, no big deal, but I have a date tomorrow night."

Odell chuckles heartily and jumps on the last car in my information train. "So Erick finally took the hint?"

A deep voice rumbles just behind me and sends a delicious tingle up my spine. "Actually, I'm hoping the honor will be all mine." Rory slips onto the stool next to me and grins expectantly.

"Yes, I'm accepting your invitation to dinner."

He smiles and nods pleasantly.

I'm happy to see he's not gloating. And when I glance up at Odell through the orders up window, his expression leans toward pleased. Which is probably the best I can hope for right now. I'm not sure how Rory got his reputation in this town, but opinions don't change overnight, especially not in almost-Canada. People seem pretty set in their ways up here.

"I only caught the tail end of that, which in my opinion was the best part, but what else is going on in your life besides a wonderful dinner tomorrow night?"

"I have a busy day, but I did solve the case."

Rory tilts his head with a little too much shock and says, "You don't say?"

I lean forward and nod meaningfully. "I do say. Maybe you haven't heard, but I have a pretty good track record." However, my shoulders droop when I think about Johan and Marguerite's situation. "To be honest, I'm actually not that happy I solved this one."

Tally slides a cup of coffee in front of me. "Nonsense. You did the right thing. And even if Ledo won't press charges, I'm certain the sheriff will."

"Well, I'm sure there's no point keeping it from you any longer. The driver's going to turn himself in this morning."

Tally steps back and swallows. "Who was it?"

I shake my head. "Unfortunately, it was Johan Olafsson. The worst part is—" I stop myself from joining the small-town gossip pool. It's one thing to tell everyone the name of the person who was driving the car; that information will be in the paper and the police report. Public knowledge. But it's not my place to share their personal business. No, my place will be to take care of setting up the rest of Marguerite's appointments. And making sure Johan's legal fees are covered by the Foundation.

Odell brings out my breakfast. "So what's this about an article for the *Post*? You writing about the case?"

I laugh a little too bitterly. "I've never been all that comfortable tooting my own horn. I'm actually writing a human-interest piece. I'm hoping Mr. Knudsen will run it on Sunday."

Odell raps his knuckles twice on the silver-flecked white counter and says, "He'd be a fool not to," before returning to the kitchen.

Rory orders a cinnamon roll and coffee while I power through my breakfast.

Eager to get on with my day, I thank Odell, bus my dishes, and accept a hug from Tally. As I'm headed toward the door a gentle reminder reaches my ear.

"Shall I pick you up at four-thirty tomorrow?"

I turn and catch just a flicker of doubt in Rory's eyes, and I smile reassuringly. "Yes, four-thirty at the bookshop. Is there any dress code?"

"I'm wearing a suit, if that helps?"

"That definitely gives— me something to go on." Once again, I almost said Grams, and one of these days I'm definitely going to slip up. With a final wave to all, I head out the front door to the hospital to give Ledo his phone. The screen is cracked, but I imagine it'll still hold a charge.

CHAPTER 24

BREAKING NEWS SATURDAY MORNING IS: "Johan Olafsson identified as hit-and-run driver that struck down Dr. Toledo Sikanen the night of the Yuletide Extravaganza."

I'm happy to report that between Doc Ledo's generosity and Erick's big heart, Johan is facing the minimum sentence of ninety days in county jail and a one-thousand-dollar fine—and we've already posted his bail. I've arranged transportation and payment for Marguerite to finish her proton-beam therapy treatments at the Mayo Clinic in Rochester. It's a shorter drive than Montreal, and should be quite a bit easier for her in the long run. Once again, I'm grateful for the Duncan-Moon Foundation.

The drive out to Stellen's house is longer than I remember, but the beauty of the snow-swept fields and ice-dusted pine trees fills the ride with splendid distractions.

Stellen chose Saturday rather than Sunday for our trip to Broken Rock, since his father spends all day in town delivering his taxidermy orders. Sunday is more of a family day, and Stellen said he's expected to be at home helping with chores. He's waiting outside when I pull up and he piles into the Jeep with an eager smile.

"Good morning, Miss Moon."

"Good morning, Stellen. And please call me Mitzy. We're friends, remember?"

He nods happily. "You don't have to buy me another statue. I mean, it's super nice and all, but I just want to say, you don't have to."

"I know. But, like I said, I really appreciated you telling me what you saw, and I know what it's like to lose your mom, you know?"

He swallows hard and nods.

The selection at the statuary center in Broken Rock is vaster than I would've imagined. As we walk down the first row, Stellen bends over and picks up a small heart-shaped stone, almost like a steppingstone.

"How about this one? This is good."

"Are you sure? I don't mean to brag, but I could

literally afford any statue in here. And, I've seen your meadow. I think it deserves a more memorable piece. Don't worry about the cost, okay? No strings attached, I promise. You already kept up your end of the deal."

He nods and sets the small stone heart back on the ground.

"Take your time. Walk up and down all the aisles and look at everything. You'll know when you find the right one."

He nods and trudges through the knee-deep snow toward the other end of the outdoor lot.

I guess it's pretty hard to shovel between all of this, or maybe they just haven't gotten around to it. As I glance up and down the rows of reindeer, moose, frogs, mushrooms, and pretty much all forms of flora and fauna, I have a warm little thought. I've never actually been to my grandmother's grave. Seeing as how she doesn't seem to be gone in my world, it never occurred to me to see where she's buried. Maybe I should find some little memento to place next to her headstone. At least it'll give me something to do while Stellen completes his search. By the time he tracks me down, most of the morning has disappeared, and despite the fact that I found a lovely marble cardinal inside the warm retail area, I've changed my mind about visiting the cemetery.

"Miss— Mitzy, I think I found something, but if it's too much, that's okay. I can find something else."

I set the little stone bird down on its shelf and whisper, "When I'm ready."

As I follow Stellen back to his discovery, I realize that no matter what he's chosen, I'll have to purchase it or I'll never have time to get back to Pin Cherry and get ready for my dinner date.

As we tramp down the row, I see various sculptures of elves, gnomes, and angels.

"Is this one okay?"

I don't even have to look at my mood ring to know that I would see an image of this statue in Stellen's memory meadow. It couldn't be more perfect. An angel crouched on one knee with his hand on the head of a beloved dog. The angel's wings are partially extended but the tips curve protectively around the dog, creating almost a heart shape from top to bottom. "I think it's perfect."

"Good. The angel's face kind of reminds me of my mom and . . . you know, the dog . . ."

"It's perfect, Stellen. A beautiful way to honor your mom and Chuckwalla. I'll tell them to load it up."

Back inside, the owner explains how I'll need a twenty-pound bag of sand to fill the base once we get it in position. I'm extremely pleased to hear that it's lighter than it looks and that the sand can be added separately, as I consider the distance from Stellen's driveway to his memory meadow. I hadn't really thought things through when I told him he could have any statue he wanted.

One thing I'm learning about my dearly departed grandmother is that she has more than a taste for finer things. Upon closer inspection, it appears that she replaced her addiction to alcohol with an addiction to wealth and haute couture. Her shoe collection aside, let me present her whole-hearted support of selecting the appropriate outfit for my date with the previously condemned Rory Bombay. Now that he's lavished me with gifts and invited me to an exclusive, upscale fine-dining establishment, all bets are off. Grams' change of heart appears to have a direct correlation to fabulous "un-cursed" emerald rings and buttery leather gloves.

"Have you finished your hair?" Grams hurtles through the wall from the closet into the bathroom and examines my attempt at a French twist.

"Oh no! Let me give it a shot." Her ability to affect material objects is definitely becoming stronger. As she pokes, prods, and smooths out my messy twisted hair, I can almost feel her touch.

"All right, dear, I've improved this as best I can and you'll have to stick one of those bobby pins right through me into this twist."

I do as I'm told, pretending not to feel the unsettling sensation of pushing my fingers through my grandmother's ghost. When I hold up the hand mirror to check my work, I have to admit Grams' magic touch—no pun intended—has improved the overall sophistication of the hairdo.

"Now, that's done. Did you use the green eye shadow palette I pointed to earlier?"

"Yes, Grams."

"Let me look at you." She carefully inspects my makeup application and nods a hesitant approval. "That'll do. Now, into the closet." She blasts through the wall while I embrace my humanity and walk around to the actual doorway.

"Silas dropped off the ring earlier and he said it's perfectly safe for you to wear. He claims the hex was amateurish, and after some brief research he simply had to ground out the energy to release the endless loop that was trapping and intensifying your powers. But if I were you, I'd leave that mood ring in our jewelry box. I don't think it's worth the risk of wearing them both together."

"Agreed." I pick up the ring off the padded mahogany bench and slip it on my right hand. The delicate cat's-eye cut emerald absolutely sparkles in the exquisite closet lighting.

"It is a lovely ring, dear. That's why I chose the emerald-green silk-velvet cocktail number by Ceil Chapman, and the Jimmy Choo patent leather platform pumps."

I examine the curve-hugging cut of the tea-length emerald-green designer dress and smirk. "That should do the trick."

"There will be no trick doing, young lady. I still have my reservations about this man and I insist that this first date include supper only."

Oh boy. Hot tears well up in the corners of my eye and Ghost-ma rushes over, fanning her ethereal hands uselessly in front of my face.

"Don't cry, sweetie. Don't cry. You'll muss your makeup. And your eyeliner is absolutely perfect. Deep breaths. Look up at the ceiling and blink slowly."

I do as I'm told and somehow managed to hold the flood of teardrops at bay.

"What's wrong? I thought you wanted to go on this date."

"I absolutely do. It's just that . . . It's just . . . you were scolding me, and making rules. I really miss my mom."

"Deep breaths. Deep breaths. Your mom would

be so proud of the beautiful young woman that you've become. One of the greatest regrets of my life, besides leaving Odell, is not having the chance to meet your mother. But we have each other, dear. Now, you blink away those tears and slip into this gorgeous dress and let me see how you look."

I have to admire Grams' ability to plumb the depths of emotion and bounce right back to fashion in the space of sixty seconds.

Nodding, I attempt to exhale all the pent-up emotion in one go.

I slip into the perfect portrait of a well-to-do heiress and for the first time in my life, use something called a "zipper hook." "That's a very handy device."

"It's an absolute must for an empowered woman of means, living on her own."

I chuckle and turn back and forth in front of the full-length mirror.

"You look smashing, Mitzy. I wish I was going along."

I slip my feet into the rather high heels and groan.

"Don't you start. As I've told you before, I can easily think of ten women who would kill to wear those shoes for five minutes."

"They're gorgeous shoes, Grams. It's just that,

well, I don't know if you've noticed—I'm a little clumsy. And these heels just mean I have farther to fall." I gesture to the six or maybe seven inches of pointy-ness.

She laughs a little too long at my expense before she replies, "A lady of your caliber is worth waiting for. Just walk slowly and purposefully. If he tries to rush you, then he's not worth it."

Somewhere in the layers of those instructions, I feel she's not actually talking about shoes, but I'm too old to be having *that* discussion.

My phone gives a startlingly loud PING, and I stare at Grams. "He's here."

"All right, put on that cashmere overcoat and tell him you will be down when you're ready."

"Lessons from the expert!" I giggle while I text my version of that message to Rory.

Grams whizzes in front of me with her hands waving wildly. "The gloves! You have to wear the gloves. A man likes to see that his gift is appreciated."

"I'm wearing the ring, Grams. I don't want to come on too strong, all right?"

"Of course, the ring is perfect. Understated, plus it shows him that it wasn't cursed."

"But it was. Wasn't it?"

"Would you like to explain to him how your alchemist-lawyer used his arcane powers to banish the gypsy's curse?"

"Well, when you put it that way." I chuckle along with Grams and blow her a kiss goodbye.

Managing the circular staircase proves tricky in the Choos, so I wisely unhook the "No Admittance" chain before exiting out the side door. Twiggy is gone for the day, and I have no one to lock up behind me if I leave through the front door.

Rory's Land Rover is parked right outside the door and he's standing at the ready with the passenger side door open. "The interior temperature is a cozy 71°F and the seat warmer is on 'three.'" He grins and winks playfully as he takes my hand and helps me into the car.

Was that an *Elf* reference? This guy might have an unexplored humorous side. This idea intrigues me.

His hand lingers on mine for a moment. "You're wearing the ring." He rubs his thumb over the beautiful stone. "What about the curse?"

I attempt to look embarrassed as I lie. "No curse. I think I had a touch of the flu. Probably caught some nasty bug when I was swimming around in that Petri dish they call a high school."

"Hmmm." He gently lays my hand in my lap and pats it, but his face doesn't display the relief I'd hoped it would.

He keeps the conversation light and the banter flirty on the drive to Grand Falls.

Regardless of his assurances, I have my doubts about a Michelin star restaurant in almost-Canada, but as soon we pull into the circular drive in front of Yves Bistro, I have to catch my breath. The entire scene is lit with a plethora of tiny, white sparkling lights and the place oozes spectacular promise.

Rory notes my expression and tosses me a few details. "The staff all wear traditional Finnish costumes, and the homestead is covered in hand-hewn wood siding. Most of the structure is original, from the late 1800s, but the wine cellar is all new construction. The original settlers would only have had a small root cellar."

"You really do love antiquities." I grin.

"Do what you love and the money will follow. Isn't that what they say?"

"They do. Whoever 'they' are."

He stops his vehicle in front of the pristine sidewalk and a young man dressed in knee-length knickerbockers, a woolen waistcoat, large squat top hat, and buckled shoes jogs around to take the keys. His "twin" steps up to open my door but Rory calls to him, "I'll assist the lady. Thanks anyway."

He walks around the vehicle, opens my door and nearly scoops me out of the Rover.

His arm feels reassuring around my waist, and

I'm grateful for the added support as I navigate the narrow steps to the front door of the renovated homestead.

Once inside, a lovely coat-check girl in a skirt, cotton blouse, vest, apron, and beribboned head-dress takes our coats.

"The restrooms are down that hallway past the mahogany sideboard."

We nod our thanks, and Rory adds, "That's an exquisite piece."

The young girl smiles vacantly. I know that look. It's the "we all have to pool our tips, so I better not blow this for the team" look.

Rory guides me toward the stairs leading to the basement wine cellar and the pre-dinner pairings.

The stairs seem to be overly authentic. The treads are narrow and the run is steep. I have to turn my feet sideways to keep from tipping right out of my Jimmy Choos.

As soon as Rory hits the last step, a very handsome Mediterranean-looking man glides over and grips his hand firmly. "Mr. Bombay! I was hoping you would return. And who is this breathtaking creature?"

I appreciate the breathtaking, but I'm not crazy about "creature."

Rory pats the man on the back with his left

hand as he draws me into the conversation. "This intelligent and fascinating woman is Mizithra Moon, of the Duncan-Moon Philanthropic Foundation."

The chef grips my right hand and raises the fingers to his lips. Before he releases his grip, he comments on my ring. "That is a stunning emerald, Miss Moon. But you truly wear *it*, not the other way around."

I'm not entirely sure I appreciate the way his eyes slide over my body like a greasy hand.

"What have you prepared for us tonight, Chef?" Rory casually inserts himself between my body and the chef's looming frame. But as soon as the topic of food is raised, the man is pure perfection. "Follow me, Mr. Bombay. Here we have a balsamic onion tartlet paired with a 1980 Samos Nectar."

After the third pairing of scrumptious bites with wines I can't pronounce, I excuse myself to use the restroom.

Two steps from the top of the stairs, a very recognizable set of broad shoulders darkens the doorway. And, true to form, my heel slips off the narrow tread, I wave my arms wildly and luckily fall forward, but unluckily smack my knee directly on the edge of the upper step.

The pain is excruciating, and it takes all my focus to keep from screaming or bawling like a baby.

Before I know what's happening, I've been scooped up as though I'm a damsel in distress, and Erick is giving orders like a medic on a battlefield.

The hostess is the first to be conscripted. "Move that arrangement off the sideboard."

A random server is next. "You, get me some ice from the kitchen. If you don't have plastic, wrap it in a dish towel." He sets me on the sideboard like a child's doll and lifts my legs up to rest parallel.

I was less embarrassed when I tripped and fell.

"Is there any chance you're here for some reason other than to rescue me?"

He takes the bag of ice from the kitchen staff and places it on my knee. "It's my mother's birthday. But let me check your ankle."

"Erick, I'm fine. Honestly. I just tripped. Nothing's broken. Seriously, this is very embarrassing."

He ignores my plea for leniency and continues his examination of my ankle. And I can't say that having his hands all over my leg is exactly a bad thing.

"I'm sure you'll have a nasty bruise on your knee, and I'm sorry about that. But I don't think you twisted your ankle." He holds up the Jimmy Choo like it's a tarantula and shakes his head as he sets it on the sideboard. "I imagine you'll be happy to know these deathtrap shoes appear to be unscathed."

His little triage center is starting to draw attention and the heat in my cheeks is from more than just his nearness.

He's right in the middle of taking one more "better safe than sorry" look at my ankle when things turn from bad to worse.

"Mitzy, what's going on?"

I'd like to say Rory's tone is all concern, but a great deal of it sounds like accusation or even resentment. Can I really blame him? I'm supposed to be on this very fancy dinner date, and somehow I've turned it into yet another opportunity for Sheriff Erick to rescue me.

"Rory, I'm so glad you're here. I tripped and fell. Extremely embarrassing. Yet not as embarrassing as all of this. Can you please get me down from here so we can continue our date?" I hope I've emphasized the word "date" enough for both of the boys to receive my meaning.

"Ah, Sheriff Harper. I suppose I should thank you for rescuing my dinner companion from a possible gangrenous infection."

Whoo, I do admire the sarcasm, although I'm sure Erick is simply acting on instinct and would much rather spend his mother's birthday with his mother.

"All part of the job, Mr. Bombay. I like to think that as sheriff, I'm never really off duty."

"You do seem to run a full-service department, Sheriff."

"I guess I'll have to get *myself* off this sideboard, eh boys?" I slip on my shoe, swing my legs down, and land gingerly on my feet, as Erick grabs my left elbow and Rory grabs the right. This evening shows no sign of improving. But at least now I feel confident in saying that things couldn't be worse.

"Ricky? Ricky, is this the lovely girl you're always talking about?"

I can practically feel the heat off Erick's face. But he doesn't even have a chance to respond before she tosses another one our way.

"My goodness! You're every bit as lovely as my Ricky says. That hair of yours! White as the driven snow!" She stares at me with a pleasant, motherly smile and adds, "And you in that dress! Breathtaking, dear. Breathtaking. Are you joining us for dinner?"

Clearly Rory is past the pleasantries and eager to restate his claim. "Good evening, Mrs. Harper, I'm Rory Bombay. I own the antiquities store in town, and Miss Moon is my dinner companion." He threads my arm through his elbow and nearly drags me downstairs.

I risk a backward glance and Erick shrugs in my general direction as he mouths the word, "Sorry."

I'd like to feel sorry, but I don't feel even a tiny bit apologetic. I'm not pleased that I tripped and fell, and made a spectacle of myself. But I've absolutely done worse this week, and it was worth it all to get the inside scoop on what "Ricky" really thinks of me. Breathtaking? That's something Erick's neglected to mention when he's telling me to mind my own business. I grin mischievously.

"Mitzy, are you actually all right? If you're injured, I'm happy to take you home and reschedule."

I better stop imagining what dating Erick could be like and start appreciating the date I'm already on. "Honestly, Rory, I'm fine. I think Erick just has a hero complex and overreacts at the slightest provocation. I tripped, which probably embarrassed him more than it hurt me, and he swooped in to save the day. I'm one hundred percent fine. I'm totally focused on enjoying my evening with my dinner companion." I smirk appropriately when I repeat his phrase and seal my promise with a little peck on his cheek.

I can assure you I do not need my mood ring to tell me how successful that gesture proves to be.

The worry evaporates from his sparkling green eyes and he smiles warmly as he scoops an arm around my waist. "I was hoping you'd say that, Miss

Moon. I'd like this to be the first of many dinners together."

I lower my eyelids demurely, but inside I'm wondering if I can successfully juggle my blossoming social life. I mean, I'm not that clumsy —right?

End of Book 3

A NOTE FROM TRIXIE

Another case solved! I'll keep writing them if you keep reading . . .

The best part of "living" in Pin Cherry Harbor has been the wonderful feedback from my early readers. Thank you to my alpha readers Angel and Michael. HUGE thanks to my fantastic beta readers who continue to give me extremely useful and honest feedback: Veronica McIntyre, Renee Arthur, and Nadine Peterse-Vrijhof. And big "small town" hugs to the world's best ARC Team – Trixie's Mystery ARC Detectives!

Much appreciation to my brilliant editor Philip Newey! Some author's dread edits, but it is always a pleasure to work with Philip, and I look forward to many more. Any errors are my own.

Now I'm writing book four in the Mitzy Moon

Mysteries series, and I think I may just live in Pin Cherry Harbor forever. Mitzy, Grams, and Pyewacket got into plenty of trouble in book one, *Fries and Alibis*. But I'd have to say that book three, *Wings and Broken Things*, is when most readers say the series becomes unputdownable.

I hope you'll continue to hang out with us.

Trixie Silvertale (December 2019)

SPARKS AND LANDMARKS

Mitzy Moon Mysteries 4

A suspicious fire. A Valentine's Day discovery. Will this psychic sleuth gamble —and lose?

Mitzy Moon's clairvoyant abilities are growing, but she never predicted arson. After waking to a towering inferno and loading her mentor into an ambulance, she thought things couldn't get worse. But when the sheriff links her father to the blaze, she's forced to take the case.

Coming up empty on love and leads pushes Mitzy to unnecessary risks. Now her otherworldly helpers, a nosy Ghost-ma and a fiendish feline, are the only ones who can save her bacon. But with break-ins, Bingo, and big storms stalling out her investigation, she may not be able to keep her dad out of jail.

Can Mitzy dig up the right clues, or will she fall for a sinister plot that puts her six feet under?

Sparks and Landmarks is the fourth book in the hilarious paranormal cozy mystery series, Mitzy Moon Mysteries. If you like snarky heroines, supernatural intrigue, and a dash of romance, then you'll love Trixie Silvertale's twisty whodunits.

Buy *Sparks and Landmarks* to light the fuse on a mystery today!

Grab yours here!
readerlinks.com/l/884696

Scan this QR Code with the camera on your phone. You'll be taken right to the Mitzy Moon Mysteries series page. You can easily grab any mysteries you've missed!

to receive updates from Pin Cherry Harbor and access to giveaways, new release announcements, behind-the-scenes secrets, and much more!

Scan this QR Code with the camera on your phone. You'll be taken right to the page to join the Club!

THANK YOU!

Trying out a new book is always a risk and I'm thankful that you rolled the dice with Mitzy Moon. If you loved the book, the sweetest thing you can do (*even sweeter than pin cherry pie à la mode*) is to leave a review so that other readers will take a chance on Mitzy and the gang.

Don't feel you have to write a book report. A brief comment like, "Can't wait to read the next book in this series!" will help potential readers make their choice.

Visit the link below to leave a quick review
https://readerlinks.com/l/803880
★★★★★

Thank you kindly, and I'll see you in Pin Cherry Harbor!

Heists and Poltergeists: Paranormal Cozy Mystery

Blades and Bridesmaids: Paranormal Cozy Mystery

Scones and Tombstones: Paranormal Cozy Mystery

Vandals and Yule Scandals: Paranormal Cozy Mystery

More to come!

MAGICAL RENAISSANCE FAIRE MYSTERIES

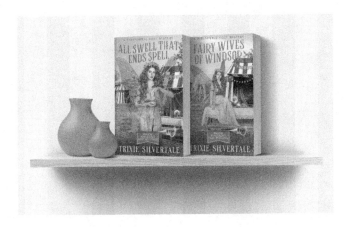

Explore the world of Coriander the Conjurer. A fortune-telling fairy with a heart of gold!

Book 1: ***All Swell That Ends Spell*** – A dubious festival. A fatal swim. Can this fortune-telling fairy herald the true killer?

Book 2: ***Fairy Wives of Windsor*** – A jolly Faire. A shocking murder. Can this furtive fairy outsmart the killer?

Join Sydney Coleman and her unruly ghosts, as they solve mysteries in a truly haunted mansion!

Book 1: **_Moonlight and Mischief_** – She's desperate for a fresh start, but is a mansion on sale too good to be true?

Book 2: **_Moonlight and Magic_** – A haunted Halloween tour seem like the perfect plan, until there's murder...

Book 3: ***Moonlight and Mayhem*** – An unwelcome visitor. A surprising past. Will her fire sale end in smoke?

ABOUT THE AUTHOR

USA TODAY Bestselling author Trixie Silvertale grew up reading an endless supply of Lilian Jackson Braun, Hardy Boys, and Nancy Drew novels. She loves the amateur sleuths in cozy mysteries and obsesses about all things paranormal. Those two passions unite in her Mitzy Moon Mysteries, and she's thrilled to write them and share them with you.

When she's not consumed by writing, she bakes to fuel her creative engine and pulls weeds in her herb garden to clear her head (*and sometimes she pulls out her hair, but mostly weeds*).

Greetings are welcome:
trixie@trixiesilvertale.com

Made in United States
Orlando, FL
13 April 2024